CLASS PETS

#1: Fuzzy's Great Escape

Bruce Hale

Scholastic Inc.

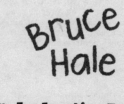

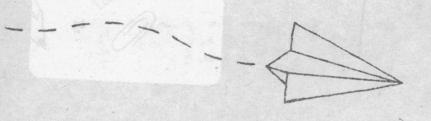

To Sharon Hearn and her cool compatriots at Children's Book World

Text and illustrations copyright © 2018 by Bruce Hale

This book is being published simultaneously in hardcover by Scholastic Press.

All rights reserved. Published by Scholastic Inc., *Publishers since 1920.* SCHOLASTIC, SCHOLASTIC PRESS, and associated logos are trademarks and/or registered trademarks of Scholastic Inc.

The publisher does not have any control over and does not assume any responsibility for author or third-party websites or their content.

No part of this publication may be reproduced, stored in a retrieval system, or transmitted in any form or by any means, electronic, mechanical, photocopying, recording, or otherwise, without written permission of the publisher. For information regarding permission, write to Scholastic Inc., Attention: Permissions Department, 557 Broadway, New York, NY 10012.

ISBN 978-1-338-14518-2

10 9 8 7 6 5 4 3

18 19 20 21 22

Printed in the U.S.A   40

First printing 2018

Book design by Baily Crawford

CONTENTS

Chapter 1: First Day, Fresh Hay   1

Chapter 2: Pets on Pillows   10

Chapter 3: Evil with a Cute Pink Nose   18

Chapter 4: Spiky Diego's Big Idea   28

Chapter 5: Cuteness Counts   35

Chapter 6: Snakes Don't Stretch   44

Chapter 7: Jailbreak Blues   54

Chapter 8: Meet the Dinos   66

Chapter 9: To Go, or Not to Go?   77

Chapter 10: A Doggy Day   87

Chapter 11: Dummying Up   96

Chapter 12: The Not-So-Great Escape   104

Chapter 13: Marta Flips Out   111

Chapter 14: Bagging It   121

Chapter 15: The Ghost with the Most   131

Chapter 16: Neanderthal Noah's Ark   143

Chapter 17: Take the Bunny and Run   154

Chapter 18: Mission: Improbable   164

Chapter 19: Showdown with Mustache   172

Chapter 20: Grime and Punishment   180

CHAPTER 1

First Day, Fresh Hay

"Look, a guinea pig!"

"Cool!"

On this first day of the new school year, Fuzzy had to hand it to the first two students through the door. These girls had their priorities in order. Pausing only to stuff their book bags into the cubbyholes, they made a beeline for his cage.

"Welcome, girls," said Miss Wills. The sweet-faced teacher had just finished setting up Room 5-B and was writing the class schedule on the blackboard. Fuzzy loved the smell of chalk almost as much as he loved the smell of fresh hay.

"Can I pick her up?" asked the first kid, who wore her dark hair in a bunch of skinny braids.

"Him," said Miss Wills. She brushed chalk dust from her palms. "And yes, you may. Gently, please."

Fuzzy tensed. For some of the newbies, *gently* meant *like a cranky sumo wrestler*. Then, two soft hands lifted him out of his cage—one wrapped around his chest, one supporting his hind legs. He relaxed. This kid knew her way around guinea pigs.

"What's his name?" asked the second girl. Her huge, blue-framed glasses gave her an owlish look.

"Fuzzy!" said Fuzzy.

The girls laughed. "He chirped," said Skinny Braids. Fuzzy had long ago gotten used to the fact that he could understand humans' language, but they couldn't understand his.

"He does that," said Miss Wills. "His name is Fuzzy."

Owl Glasses giggled. "That's a funny name."

"Tell me about it," squeaked Fuzzy. He would've preferred something more macho, like Rex, Rocky, or Hulk. But the class that named him had really admired his fur—and that class had a particularly pink-and-frilly ringleader, a girl named Shakira, who nominated the name. And so he was Fuzzy forevermore.

"He sure talks a lot," said Skinny Braids.

Miss Wills smiled. "Fuzzy likes being part of the conversation."

This was true. Fuzzy had *lots* of ideas, and he was eager to share them. In fact, he considered himself an Idea Rodent. Unfortunately, not everyone wanted to hear his ideas—the other class pets, for example.

But all that was about to change.

As the girls fussed over him and more students wandered in, Fuzzy thought about how this new school year would be different. For two whole years, he'd longed to be president of the Class Pets Club, but twice over, the other pets had elected Geronimo the rat.

Not anymore.

Sly old Geronimo had retired to a farm over the summer, and Fuzzy knew what that meant. Tonight, at the year's first Class Pets Club meeting, he would finally achieve his dream. President Fuzzy! It had a nice ring to it.

Then the other pets would listen to his great ideas. Oh, the adventures they'd have!

Wheek! An eager whistle squeaked out of him. Owl Glasses nearly dropped Fuzzy in surprise.

"Okay, girls," said Miss Wills, coming to the rescue. "Fuzzy's had enough excitement for now, and it's time to start class."

But even back in his cage, Fuzzy couldn't contain himself. He raced up and down, hopping in the air. *Wheek, wheek!*

The new students laughed and applauded. As well they might. For this, he knew, would be his year. The Year of Fuzzy. He couldn't wait for tonight.

So, of course, he had to wait.

Through the introductions of all the new students, shy and brassy, eager and reluctant. Through the vote on the classroom rules for the year. Through his own introduction to this fresh crop of fifth graders.

But Fuzzy didn't resent the wait. He took his job as class pet seriously. The way Fuzzy saw it, his duty was to inspire and encourage his new friends. How else would they learn, but from an experienced pet like himself?

That meant tamping down his excitement to reassure Nervous Lily, and enduring Heavy-Handed Jake's clumsiness. It also meant keeping quiet when Miss Wills read from one of Fuzzy's favorite books, *Stuart Little*.

Still, Fuzzy breathed a sigh of relief at the end of the day. Finally, Miss Wills gave him his farewell snuggles. Then she turned off the lights, said "Good night, sweet Fuzzy," and locked the door.

At last, his evening could begin!

As the *tok-tok-tok* of Miss Wills's heels faded down the hallway, Fuzzy went to work on escaping his cage. Leaning his full weight against the plastic platform, he dug in his hind legs and push-push-pushed until it bumped up against the wire wall.

Next, he retrieved his ball from the corner and nosed it over until it nudged the platform. Finally, Fuzzy shoved a wooden block beside the ball. He stepped back to check it out. Perfect!

"After all, I may not be the world's best fence climber," he told himself, "but any old rodent can climb stairs."

He scrambled on top of the block. Easy peasy. Fuzzy braced his front paws on the ball. So far, so good. But when he brought his back paws up . . .

Yikes! The ball rolled sideways!

Fuzzy scrabbled the opposite way with all four feet, barely keeping his balance. The ball slowed . . .

Then it reversed direction. "Who-o-o-oah!"

And just at that moment, a key clattered in the lock, and the classroom door swung open.

Fuzzy teetered. Fuzzy tottered. Then . . .

Whoomph! Down he fell onto the pine shavings.

A tall man in brown coveralls stepped into the room. Flicking on the lights, he strode across to the open-topped cage and peered in. The rich smell of butterscotch drifted on his breath. "Hey, you okay, little buddy?" he asked.

"Just fine." Fuzzy scrambled back onto his feet.

Wiggling whiskers, that was close! He'd completely forgotten about Darius Poole. Every afternoon like clockwork, the janitor tidied up the classrooms. What if he'd caught Fuzzy running around outside the cage? That could've meant the end of Fuzzy's big plans.

"Trying to balance on your ball?" asked Mr. Darius. His long face hovered over the cage like a blimp with stubble. "Not as easy as it looks. Hey, you know how you get to Carnegie Hall?"

"Um, walk?" said Fuzzy.

"Practice, practice, practice." The janitor gave a low chuckle at his own joke.

Fuzzy liked how Mr. Darius talked to him, man to rodent. Though he knew it wasn't possible, sometimes he'd almost swear that the janitor understood his chirps and squeaks.

"Here, this'll keep up your strength," said Mr. Darius. He dug into one of his pockets, producing an apple slice. Was it any wonder that the janitor ranked as one of the class pets' all-time favorite humans? The man knew what a pet needed.

Fuzzy munched on the fruit while Mr. Darius swept the room and emptied the wastebaskets. It didn't take long. After the janitor turned out the lights and said, "Good night, little buddy," Fuzzy waited.

And waited.

Guinea pigs aren't championship waiters.

Finally, when he couldn't stand it anymore, Fuzzy made his move. Back into position went the ball—braced by a second block this time. Then, *bimp-bomp-bump*, up and over the wall he went.

A free guinea pig at last!

CHAPTER 2

Pets on Pillows

Not for nothing was Geronimo the rat elected Class Pets president two times running. After all, he'd made it possible for the Class Pets Club to happen in the first place.

Without Geronimo, nobody but Luther the boa constrictor would have discovered how to escape their cages. Without Geronimo, nobody would've found the forgotten space above Room 2-B's closet that ended up becoming their secret clubhouse.

Fuzzy thought about the wily rat as he scrambled down from his cage, following the route Geronimo had shown him. Across the room, and up onto the cubbyholes. Along the plastic saguaro cactus, onto the bookshelf. Then up, up, up, all the way to the top.

There, Fuzzy paused for a moment, panting. Escape was hard work! He deserved a treat, but all the food was far below. He shook his head. Such a shame.

After catching his breath, around the globe he went, then up over the stack of board games that nobody ever played, to stand beneath the loose ceiling tile. A little heave-ho on tiptoe, a mad scramble, and Fuzzy found himself in the crawl space above.

It was dark; it was deserted. It smelled like plywood and peanut butter.

Fuzzy always found this space a little creepy. Okay, a *lot* creepy. Still, if he wanted to lead the pets, he had to be brave. Fuzzy shook himself and headed toward Room 2-B, his paws sending up puffs of dust with each step.

The dust billowed, tickling his nose. His whiskers twitched. Fuzzy tried to clamp down his nostrils. *Must keep quiet. Can't make a—*

"Ah-ah-ah-*chooo!*" Fuzzy's sneeze exploded in the stillness.

He froze. He listened. Had Mr. Darius heard? Had someone else noticed?

Faint birdsong penetrated from outdoors. Roof timbers creaked. Other than that, nothing.

Fuzzy let out a long, long breath. When he was double-sure that nobody had overheard him, he began to move again. Above the row of classrooms he went, heading for the lower grades. As he walked, Fuzzy began composing his acceptance speech. "This is a victory, not just for me, but for all the pets of—"

At the start of the second-grade block, something scuttled in the darkness. Fuzzy stiffened. All his hairs stood on end. "Who's there?"

"Nobody!" squeaked a high voice.

"Mistletoe?" said Fuzzy. "Is that you?"

"N-nope." The voice quavered. "N-no Mistletoe here."

Fuzzy relaxed, smiling. "Mistletoe, I know your voice."

"Oh." A pause. "Fuzzy, is that you?"

He crept forward, careful not to startle her. In the dim spill of light that leaked around a ceiling tile, Fuzzy saw the petite shape of Room 3-A's pet, Mistletoe the mouse. Her cocoa-brown eyes were huge with alarm.

"See? No need to worry," said Fuzzy.

Mistletoe pursed her lips. "Can't be too careful. I heard Room 6-C has a new pet."

"Geronimo's replacement?" said Fuzzy.

The mouse glanced around the crawl space, lowering her voice. "It could be another *snake*." She shivered.

"Luther's not so bad," said Fuzzy, "for a boa."

"A snake is a snake." Mistletoe nodded meaningfully. "And to a snake, every mouse is a meal."

Fuzzy elbowed her. "Lighten up, Doom Girl. He'd never eat a fellow pet."

"I don't know . . ."

"Not while I'm president," said Fuzzy. "Um, I do have your vote, don't I?"

The mouse gave him a thumbs-up. "Abso-tutely!"

"Thanks," said Fuzzy. "Now, let's hurry. The next Class Pets president can't be late to his own election."

Together they hustled along until they stood over Room 2-B. Buttery-yellow light shone upward where a ceiling tile lay askew. The murmur of voices reached them.

Mistletoe tensed, hanging back. "Er, you go first," she said. "Just in case."

Fuzzy led the way to the hatch, where the end of a long plank peeked out. He began strolling down it slowly, with dignity, as an almost-president should. But when Mistletoe joined him, their combined weight made the board bounce.

Wooga wooga wooga.

"Careful!" cried Fuzzy, staggering forward.

"I can't stop!" said the mouse.

"Holy haystacks!"

The pair stumbled, then scrambled, then skidded down the plank.

"Ahhhh!"

Ka-thomp! They landed in a heap, with Mistletoe's tail draped across Fuzzy's nose like an upside-down mustache.

Laughter greeted them. Fuzzy blinked, peering about. Most of the other pets had already arrived and were lounging around their clubhouse.

"Honestly," said Igor the green iguana. "You just *have* to make a big entrance, don't you?" He sprawled against one of the little pillows borrowed from Mr. Chopra's room, nibbling on a grape.

Mistletoe bounded to her feet. "Wowza-yowza! I

thought we were going to die! But we're not dead, are we? I'm glad."

Burning with embarrassment, Fuzzy stood and brushed himself off. "I, uh, always meant to try that," he said. "Nice slide."

"Happy new school year, dear," said Marta. A wrinkled old Russian tortoise, she attended only some of the club's meetings. Hauling that shell around took a fair bit of effort. "Such an exciting day, isn't it?"

"Today?" said Fuzzy, trying to act casual. "Oh yeah. Isn't this the day we elect a new Class Pets president? I'd almost forgotten."

Igor smirked. "*Sure* you had."

Fuzzy surveyed the room. It was a warm, cozy space, furnished with borrowed pillows and knickknacks, and lit by stolen candles. Besides Marta and Igor, Luther the rosy boa had also showed up.

Wrapped around a crooked cat sculpture Geronimo had saved from a wastebasket, the snake gave the newcomers a sleepy smile. "What's happenin', Fuzzarino?" His grin widened. "Hello, Mistletoe. Mi*ssss* me?"

The mouse gulped, edging behind Fuzzy. "Luther," she squeaked.

Fuzzy glanced over at the president's podium, a fat copy of *The Complete Works of William Shakespeare*. Geronimo had dragged that up too, despite weighing far less than the massive book.

The podium was empty. But not for long. Soon, Fuzzy would claim his rightful place.

"So, is this everyone?" he asked. "Can we get started?"

"Hold up awhile," said Luther. "Sassafras went to tell the new pet about our meeting."

"They'll be here soon," said Marta.

Soon? Fuzzy shifted from foot to foot. He had a feeling *soon* meant something different to an animal that could live over forty years and took ten minutes just to cross her cage.

But as it turned out, he didn't have long to wait. With an earsplitting squawk and a flutter of orange and green feathers, Sassafras the parakeet glided down into the clubhouse.

"It's showtime!" she screeched. "How's everybody doing tonight?"

"Um, fine?" said Mistletoe.

Sassafras spread her wings wide. "Well, hold on to

your hats, ladies and germs, because it's my pleasure to introduce the newest member of our Class Pets Club. Yes, she's the toast of Room 6-C, our very own . . . Miss Cinnabun!"

As one, the animals turned and craned their necks to look up the ramp. When Fuzzy saw who waited there, his jaw dropped in astonishment.

CHAPTER 3

Evil with a Cute Pink Nose

She glided slowly and serenely down the plank. Not tumbling like Fuzzy, not swooping like Sassafras, but *gliding* like a human on an escalator. Her fur was as fluffy as a baby cloud. Her ears were long and floppy. Her eyes twinkled like starlight, and her nose was the pinkest, most perfect thing anyone had ever seen.

Fuzzy mistrusted the bunny on sight. Nobody was this perfect.

"I do declare," Cinnabun drawled as she stepped off the ramp, "what a fine-looking group of pets you are."

Suddenly bashful, Mistletoe hid her face.

The bunny beamed, hopping around to greet each of

them in turn. "Y'all have such a lovely clubhouse. I so appreciate your inviting me to join you."

Luther the boa smiled back. "The pleasure is ours, Missy Miss."

When even sarcastic Igor said, "Delighted to meet you," Fuzzy's eyes nearly bugged out. Igor wasn't delighted to meet anyone.

What was going on?

"Can we get you a PowerBar?" said Mistletoe. She scurried over to the corner and dragged back a snack that she'd lifted from the school vending machine. "It's from May—or April, maybe—but these things last forever."

"You're too kind," said Cinnabun. She nibbled on the bar. "Mmm, I feel more powerful already."

The pets chuckled. Fuzzy rolled his eyes.

"So what do y'all do at these meetings?" asked the bunny.

"Gossip about teachers," said Igor, munching another grape.

"Eat snacks!" squeaked Mistletoe.

Marta raised her head. "And at this particular meeting, we elect our president for the year."

"That's right," said Fuzzy, "and I—"

"Fascinating," cooed Cinnabun. "Can absolutely anyone be president?"

"Anyone with a pulse," squawked Sassafras. "Guess that leaves you out, Luther."

The boa lifted a brow. "Ha, ha."

"And what kind of qualities should a president have?" asked Cinnabun, toying with one of her floppy ears.

"Leadership," said Marta.

"Charm," said Mistletoe, with a shy smile at the bunny.

"Good ideas, experience, and a real knowledge of this school," said Fuzzy. Something about this conversation had him on edge.

Sassafras pointed a wing feather at the rabbit. "Hey," she said, "*you* have all those qualities. Why don't you be our next president?"

"*What?*" squeaked Fuzzy. He couldn't believe his ears.

Cinnabun's nose twitched adorably. "Little ol' me? The new kid? Oh, I couldn't possibly . . ."

"That's not how we—" Fuzzy began.

"Great idea," said Mistletoe. "Let's take a vote. All in favor?"

"Aye!" thundered all the animals except Fuzzy.

"But I—" he said.

Marta the tortoise extended a wrinkled front foot to the bunny. "Congratulations," she said, "Madam President."

"I—I—I," Fuzzy spluttered. Words jammed in his throat like alphabet blocks in a drain. A roaring sound filled his ears, and his knees wobbled.

Bubbling with congratulations, the other pets crowded around Cinnabun. They shook her paw, patted her shoulder, and marveled at her silky-smooth fur.

"You'll make a tippety-top president," said Mistletoe. "You're just what we need."

"About time we had a girl in charge," said Sassafras. "Right on, sister!"

"Wait!" someone cried. Everyone turned to look at who'd spoken, and with a start, Fuzzy realized it was him.

"Something wrong, ace?" hissed Luther the boa.

Now that he had their attention, Fuzzy's ears tingled and his throat felt tighter than the sweater vest the students made him wear last Christmas.

"Uh, I—that is, we . . ." He took a deep breath. "It all happened so fast."

"What did?" asked Marta with a slow blink.

"The vote."

Scratching his back on the presidential podium, Igor said, "Fast is good. Some of us have short life spans."

"But what if other candidates wanted to run?" said Fuzzy.

"Like who?" asked Marta.

Fuzzy swallowed. "Like me."

Mistletoe studied the floor.

The boa shrugged, and the motion rippled down his thick body. "Majority rules, dude. Everybody voted for Missy Miss except you. That's five to one."

Holding up her paws, Cinnabun said, "Just a moment, please. I never intended to cause conflict in the club. If y'all would like to hold a revote—"

"Absolu—" Fuzzy began.

"Too late!" squawked Sassafras. "The people have spoken!"

"But we're animals," Fuzzy objected.

"Doesn't matter. A vote's a vote," said the parakeet.

Dimples sprouted at either end of Cinnabun's smile. "Far be it from me to disappoint the voters. I accept the presidency."

"Yay!" cheered all the pets but one.

"She doesn't even know our school," said Fuzzy. "It's her first day."

"And look how much she's accomplished already," said Mistletoe. "Can you imagine what she'll have done after her first week?"

Fuzzy tugged his whiskers in frustration. "A president should have big ideas. Am I the only one who cares that we haven't heard a single idea from her?"

"Yes," said Igor, Luther, and Sassafras together.

"Now, now," said Cinnabun. "The pig has a point."

"Uh, actually I'm a rodent and—" Fuzzy began.

The bunny spoke over him. "I *am* new to this school, and I *haven't* told y'all my intentions as president. So that's why my term will begin with a listening tour."

"What's that?" asked Sassafras.

Hopping gracefully up onto the podium, Cinnabun said, "I will listen to all of *y'all's* ideas, and learn what's in your hearts and minds before I try leading you."

The class pets cheered.

"Smart and sure-footed too," murmured Mistletoe.

Fuzzy gnawed his lip. He wished he'd thought of the listening tour. He wished he'd forced the pets to vote before Cinnabun arrived. He wished that Leo Gumpus Elementary had banned floppy-eared bunnies for all eternity.

Through a haze, he watched Cinnabun chatter and the other animals gaze at her with dopey grins. What a phony. She could talk all she wanted about listening, but Fuzzy bet that she'd totally ignore him. Why, she—

"—about you?"

Fuzzy started. Cinnabun was looking directly at him.

"Huh?" He noticed all the others were staring too.

"Despite all appearances," drawled Igor, "he really does have a brain."

"What were we talking about?" asked Fuzzy.

"I was saying," Cinnabun said, "that you seem to have plenty of opinions. So why don't I start my listening tour with you?"

Fuzzy watched her warily. Was she mocking him?

The bunny gazed down with liquid brown eyes, the soul of sincerity.

"Well, um . . ." He cleared his throat. "Okay. Last year, I noticed the students leaving on these one-day adventures—to the zoo, the museum, or a concert."

"Field trips," said Marta wisely.

Fuzzy nodded. "Exactly. And the kids were always so excited when they came back. So full of stories about all the cool things they saw and did. And I thought that I—I mean, we . . ."

He looked at the faces around him. Igor, skeptical. Luther, sleepy. Sassafras, suspicious.

"Ah, forget it," said Fuzzy.

"Wait till you hear *my* ideas," said Igor. "I think we ought to—"

Holding up a paw, Cinnabun said, "Brother Igor, please. It's only polite that we hear Brother Pig—"

"The name's Fuzzy," muttered Fuzzy.

The bunny blinked. "Really? That's an . . . unusual name for a boy."

"Yeah," said Fuzzy. "I know."

"It's only polite that we hear Brother Fuzzy's ideas," said Cinnabun. She turned those melty chocolate eyes on him again. "Do continue."

Fuzzy took a deep breath. "Well, we never get to

see the outside world, except when a student babysits us on the weekend. So I thought, why can't we have an adventure together? A Class Pets Club field trip?"

Igor scoffed. Mistletoe nibbled her lip. Luther and Sassafras traded a glance.

Fuzzy's heart sank. Not only did he not get to be president, but his fellow pets hated his favorite idea. He was a foolish rodent to think he could dream big and get away with it. Dumb, dumb, dumb. Fuzzy slumped, turning away.

And then, Cinnabun said, "I think that's an excellent idea!"

"You do?" said Fuzzy.

"You do?" said Igor.

"I do," said the rabbit. "And as president of the Class Pets Club, I appoint you, Brother Fuzzy, to plan our first field trip!"

CHAPTER 4

Spiky Diego's Big Idea

"Where will we go? What will we do? Will there be cats? Will it be safe?" Mistletoe peppered Fuzzy with questions as they headed back to their home classrooms after the meeting.

"I have no idea," said Fuzzy. "I haven't picked a place yet." He scowled, remembering her earlier actions. "By the way, thanks for having my back. Whatever happened to 'I'm abso-tutely voting for you'?"

Mistletoe ducked her head. "I'm so sorry, Fuzzy. But you know me."

"Do I?"

She wrung her paws. "It's just—that bun-bun was so pretty, and she talked so nice, and before I knew it, I was nominating her for president."

Fuzzy grunted.

"*Please* don't be mad," said the mouse. "Pretty, pretty please?"

Dodging around a duct in the crawl space, Fuzzy considered. He couldn't stay mad at Mistletoe. She was who she was—timid, excitable, easily swayed. Might as well get mad at a ball for bouncing.

He heaved a heavy sigh. "Don't worry about it."

The mouse's expression of relief was almost comical. "Thankyou-thankyou-thankyou," she gushed, grabbing his paw and pumping it. "You're the best!"

And with a flick of her tail, Mistletoe spun and slipped through a gap in the ceiling tile, into Room 3-A. "See you at the next meeting!" came her muffled squeak.

Dazed and distracted, Fuzzy shuffled along to his own room, wondering what had just happened. The presidency had been his for the taking. It had been close enough to taste. How had he missed out?

Cinnabun.

It was all the fault of that ridiculous rabbit. With her perfect fur and her pretty-pretty eyes and her disgusting charm. Fuzzy chuffed, kicking a duct in frustration.

"Ow!" Shaking his paw, he hobbled onward, mocking the new president in a snarky voice. " 'Far be it from me to disappoint the voters.' Dumb bunny."

He'd show her. He'd take the pets on the most amazing field trip ever. In fact, it would be so mind-blowingly awesome, they would immediately fire Cinnabun and make him president in her place. They'd see what a *real* president could do.

Just one teeny-tiny problem stood in his way:

Where would they go on the field trip?

Over the next two days, Fuzzy spent all his spare time wrestling with this challenge. It couldn't be just any old field trip. It had to be the best one ever.

While he helped his class with geography (*Where do guinea pigs come from?*), Fuzzy puzzled and plotted. While he taught the kids math (*How much does a guinea pig weigh?*), he fretted and fussed.

The zoo sounded like fun, based on what Zoey-with-the-braces had told her friends before school. But where the heck was it? And how did you get there?

According to Loud Brandon, the water park was "twenty types of awesome." But Fuzzy wasn't sure all the class pets could swim as well as he could. And he sure couldn't picture perfect Madam President getting her silky fur all wet.

A concert, maybe? Maybe not. Based on the time his class took Fuzzy along to their school band practice, he thought the whole thing sounded kind of screechy and boomy.

At lunchtime on the second day, Fuzzy sat gnawing on a corner of his block, thinking. Every idea he'd come up with had a flaw in it, and the pets' meeting was happening in just a few hours. He needed the perfect field trip spot, and he needed it quickly.

In the end, the answer came from an unexpected place: his teacher, Miss Wills.

Near the end of lunch period, Miss Wills unlocked the door and began grading papers while waiting for the kids to return. First in was Spiky Diego. Fuzzy thought he had the most interesting hair of all the boys in class.

It leaned in from the sides of his head, forming a bristly crest that ran from front to back, almost like Igor the iguana's spikes.

It looked cool. It looked tough. Fuzzy wished *his* hair would do that.

Leaning over the cage, Diego gave Fuzzy a couple of gentle strokes. "Hey, Miss Wills," he said. "Do you need any help with Fuzzy? I'm really good with pets."

She looked up from the homework papers and put down her red pen. "Are you really?"

"Yep." Spiky Diego puffed up his chest. "Back home in California, we had hamsters, bunnies, three cats, two dogs, and a leopard gecko. But we only got to keep the dogs and the gecko when we moved here."

Standing, Miss Wills approached the cage. "Thanks for offering. We usually assign those tasks at the end of the first week. But since you're the first one to speak up . . ."

Diego bounced on the balls of his feet. "Ooh, what can I do?"

The teacher smiled down at Fuzzy. "Our friend is looking a little thirsty today. Can I count on you to make sure he has fresh, clean water?"

"Every single day," said Spiky Diego.

Fuzzy checked his water bowl. It wasn't the neatest. In fact, now that he considered it, the bowl was half-full of pine shavings and pellets. How on earth had that happened? *Wasn't me*, he thought.

Diego emptied the water bowl and refilled it while Miss Wills tidied up the cage a bit. Fuzzy purred. He liked having housekeeping service.

Fuzzy half listened as Diego talked about some of the things he missed from California—the weather, the Dodgers games, even the farmers' markets.

"But we have farmers' markets here," said Miss Wills. "During the warmer months, anyway."

Diego's eyes lit up. "Really? With cheese booths, and street musicians, and everything?"

"Of course," said Miss Wills. "In fact, there's one on Thursday after school not five minutes away. They cordon off three blocks of Preston Street."

"For real?" said Diego, placing the clean water bowl back in the cage.

The teacher chuckled. "All the fresh fruits and veggies you can eat."

Wheek-wheek! Fuzzy whistled and jumped up, almost upsetting his bowl.

"Whoa, big fella," said Miss Wills. "Looks like somebody else likes the farmers' market."

"No kidding!" squeaked Fuzzy.

Laughing, Miss Wills and Spiky Diego took their seats. Soon, the rest of the students had returned and resumed their lessons. But in his cage, Fuzzy practically vibrated with excitement.

All the fresh fruits and veggies you can eat? Wiggling whiskers!

He purred louder. It sounded like he'd just found his first field trip.

CHAPTER 5

Cuteness Counts

"I don't think so," said Igor, after Fuzzy had made his report at the Class Pets Club meeting a few hours later. "I already get all the fresh greens I can eat, without leaving the comfort of my own cage."

"Where's your sense of adventure?" said Fuzzy. "Don't you want to see the world, try new things?"

Igor sniffed. "I tried broccoli once. Didn't care for it."

Fuzzy turned to the rest of the pets. Most lounged on pillows around the clubhouse, nibbling nuts and fruit sticks that Mistletoe had liberated from the vending machine. "What about you guys?" he asked. "Who's up for an adventure?"

"I'm worried we'll get lost," moaned Marta the tortoise. "Do we even know where Preston Street is?"

Fuzzy waved her off. "No problem. Sassafras can fly ahead and scout it out."

"And what if we meet savage cats?" said Mistletoe, pacing. "Or hawks? Or hungry badgers?"

"It's a city," said Fuzzy. "There aren't any badgers." He ground his teeth together. What was wrong with his fellow pets? Didn't anyone want to explore?

"Well, I like the idea," said Luther. "I'm always up for a little look-see. Check out new places, eat new food*sss* . . ." He cast a teasing glance at the mouse.

Mistletoe shuddered. "That's what I'm afraid of."

"Count me in," said Sassafras the parakeet. "Bright lights, big city!"

From her perch on the presidential podium, Cinnabun twitched her pert pink nose. "I want to thank all of y'all for expressing your opinions. That's the foundation of our democracy. Now, if there's no further discussion . . . ?" She looked around.

Igor shrugged.

"All in favor?" asked the bunny.

Fuzzy raised a paw, Sassafras lifted a wing, and Luther held up his tail.

"Opposed?"

Mistletoe and Igor raised their paws, while Marta lifted a foot.

"Mercy me, a deadlock," said Cinnabun. "Now, it falls to me, as the cutest president at Leo Gumpus"—she dimpled prettily and batted her eyes—"to cast the deciding vote. And I vote . . ."

Fuzzy bit his knuckle. Which way would she go? Would the bunny-in-chief shoot down his dreams?

". . . In favor of this field trip," said Cinnabun. She rapped the presidential gavel—a rubber mallet borrowed from the kindergarten—against the Shakespeare book. "The motion is carried!"

Hardly able to believe his ears, Fuzzy cheered. Sassafras too. Luther said, "Crazy, man!" The other pets exchanged nervous glances.

"Does everyone have to go?" the mouse asked.

"Of course," said Fuzzy.

"Well, I shouldn't think so," said Cinnabun over him. "After all, this expedition is supposed to be fun. If you'd rather sit this one out—"

"Yes, please!" Mistletoe squeaked.

"Then I'm sure none of us will hold it against you."

Fuzzy frowned.

"I'm out too," said Igor, gnawing on a fruit chew. "I let my humans do all my shopping."

"Fine," said Fuzzy. "But don't come crying to me when you hear about all those yummy greens we eat."

The iguana sent him a dirty look.

Clapping her paws, Cinnabun said, "It's settled, then. Everyone who's going, meet here tomorrow for our first field trip. And now . . ." She glanced around, an expectant expression on her face. "I have a surprise."

Mistletoe perked up. "Goody! I love surprises. Is it a blueberry muffin?"

"Not this time," said the bunny. "But it is rather sweet. Having finished my listening tour and gotten to know all you lovely pets . . ."

She beamed at the group, and even Fuzzy found himself smiling back before he stopped himself.

". . . I've come up with a new tradition for this club."

Excited murmurs broke out. Fuzzy narrowed his eyes. What exactly did she have in mind?

"Starting today, the Class Pets Club will hold a weekly cuteness contest!" Cinnabun squealed.

"Splendiddly!" chirped Mistletoe.

"It's on!" squawked Sassafras. "I can out-cute anyone."

The rest of the pets traded dubious looks. Fuzzy scowled. *Cute?* What self-respecting boar guinea pig wanted to be cute? Macho, maybe. Handsome, sure.

But cute?

"Not fair," said Igor.

"Why not?" asked Sassafras.

"Nobody thinks iguanas are cute. This contest is antireptile."

The bunny flapped a paw at him. "Aw, cheer up, Mr. Grumpypants! Everybody can be cute, given the chance."

Luther raised a skeptical brow. "Everybody?"

"I swear on a stack of Barbies," said Cinnabun. "Now here's how it works. First, everybody form a circle, so we can all see each other's sweet faces."

The pets moved into position, nudging pillows out of the way.

"We'll go around, one by one," said Cinnabun. "Show us your cutest, most adorable expression, and after everyone has had their turn, we'll pick a winner."

Fuzzy turned to Luther. "Are boas cute?"

"Not so's you'd notice," said the snake.

Clasping her paws to her cheek, Cinnabun said, "This is going to be amazing! All right now, Sister Marta. Show us what cuteness is all about."

Marta blinked doubtfully. The old tortoise tried to arrange her features in a smile, but to be honest, it looked more like a bad case of gas.

The iguana snorted.

"Simply lovely," said Cinnabun. "Now you, Sister Sassafras."

"I got this," said the bird. She ruffled her feathers, grinned widely, and cocked her head right, then left. "Ta-da!"

"So, so adorable," said the bunny. "I can see why parakeets are such popular pets. Brother Igor?"

"Huh?" said the iguana, who had finally demolished his fruit stick.

"Your turn."

With a heavy sigh, Igor showed his deadpan, pre-historic face around the circle. "Happy?"

"Yes, uh, very interesting," said Cinnabun.

"Ooh, I'm next," said Mistletoe. She ducked her head, looked up from under at the other animals, then twitched her nose.

"Charming." Marta sighed.

"Yes, very," said Cinnabun with a slight edge to her voice. As Fuzzy saw it, Mistletoe was the bunny's toughest competition in the cuteness department.

"Brother Fuzzy?" said Cinnabun.

"Oh, all right," he said. Plastering on a fake smile, he raised his paws beside his face and said, "Cute, cute, cute. Are we done yet?"

"Almost," said Cinnabun. "I'll go after Brother Luther."

"I'll pa*ssss*," said the snake.

Cinnabun aimed her dimples at him. "Now don't be such a sourpuss. Everyone takes a turn. It's a morale builder!"

"If you insist."

Rearing up so he swayed above the other animals, the boa wore his usual serious expression. Then, ever so slowly, he unfurled a sinister smile, the kind that said *You're my lunch* without actually saying a word.

Sassafras gasped. Mistletoe hid behind Igor, and even Cinnabun shuddered a little. "That's . . . uh, remarkable," she said.

"My morale may never recover," said Fuzzy.

"Brother Luther, maybe something a little more like *this*." The bunny composed herself. She dropped her head, like an actor getting into character, and then she raised it. Pure, 24-karat adorability shone

from her like warmth from the sun. Her eyes twinkled, her smile caressed, and her floppy ears looked extra floppy.

A great "Awww" rose from the pets. Mistletoe broke into applause, followed by the others, except for Luther, who had no paws, and Fuzzy, who was trying to control his gag reflex.

"You're the cutest ever!" the pets cried.

Suddenly bashful, Cinnabun hid her face, but she quickly recovered. "Thank you," she said. "Thank y'all so much! I simply don't know what to say."

Several of the pets crowded around to congratulate their president. Over their compliments, Fuzzy heard her say, "Now wasn't that fun-fun-fun?"

"Like a case of chiggers," muttered Igor.

Fuzzy snorted. "You voted for her."

"Sure," said the iguana, "before anyone mentioned cuteness contests."

Shaking his head, Fuzzy turned away. This was President Cinnabun in action? He thought he might go stark-raving bonkers and pull out his whiskers one by one.

It was going to be a long, long year.

CHAPTER 6

Snakes Don't Stretch

The next day, Fuzzy listened closely to Miss Wills and her students, but heard nothing more about the farmers' market. He wished he knew how to research it on the classroom computer. But sadly, that was beyond his guinea piggy abilities.

Of course, he could imagine it. After all, he knew what farmers were, and he'd seen a market that time when Miss Wills stopped there after the vet's office. So Fuzzy pictured the farmers' market as a huge building with lots of little farms inside it. He wasn't quite sure why anyone would want to create that, but humans did all kinds of strange and amazing things. Far be it for a guinea pig to second-guess them.

Fuzzy didn't know how to break out of school and reach the market without being seen. But he wasn't worried. They'd figure it out when the time came. He was more focused on those vast quantities of fresh, delicious veggies, all ripe for the sampling.

By the time afternoon arrived, Fuzzy was so keyed up, he'd worn a groove in his pine-shaving floor from pacing back and forth. When the final bell rang and the students rose to go, he hopped up and down.

Adventure at last!

"Fuzzy likes it when school's out!" Zoey-with-the-braces giggled.

"Yeah," said Heavy-Handed Jake. "I bet he's got a hot date."

Zoey swatted his arm and giggled some more. "Guinea pigs don't date, silly."

They joined the flow of kids heading out the door, and soon the room fell quiet. After another half hour, Miss Wills packed up her papers and purse. Removing a chunk of cucumber from a container in the minifridge, she strolled over to the cage and dropped it in.

Fuzzy pounced on it.

"Be good, little guy," she said, giving him one last snuggle. Fuzzy cringed guiltily, but she didn't notice. The teacher collected her things, turned off the lights, and locked the door.

After Mr. Darius came to tidy up, Fuzzy waited as long as he could for the coast to be clear. It wasn't long. By the time the janitor was working on Room 5-C, Fuzzy had set up his ball and blocks, and was making his escape.

As he climbed the cubbyholes and bookshelf, he started reciting the names of all the vegetables he planned to sample at the farmers' market.

"Arugula and cabbage, watercress and chicory," he half sang as he climbed. "Parsnips, peppers, and peas. This will be epic!"

Fuzzy trotted through the crawl space in record time. His nerves buzzed with anticipation, leaving him feeling like he was wearing a coat made of ants.

At last, he scooted down the plank and into the clubhouse. "Here I am! Who's ready for a field trip?"

Fuzzy looked around. Only Sassafras, Luther, and Cinnabun waited for him.

"No one else?" he asked. He'd hoped Mistletoe might change her mind.

"This is it," said Sassafras.

"All ready for our first big adventure," said Cinnabun.

Luther grinned. "So what's the plan, Stan?"

Rubbing his paws together, Fuzzy said, "We break out of school, walk to the farmers' market, eat and look around, and then we come back."

The bunny blinked. "I was expecting a little more detail."

"Detail?" said Fuzzy. "Like what?"

She scratched an ear thoughtfully with a hind paw. "Like . . . *Where* do we break out? How do we keep from being seen? What happens if we get separated? That sort of thing."

Fuzzy frowned. It had never occurred to him that field trips would require this kind of fancy planning. He flapped a paw. "It's an adventure," he said. "Part of the fun is figuring it out as we go along."

"Well," said Cinnabun. "If you're sure."

"Sure I'm sure." Fuzzy tried to sound confident. He turned to the boa. "Hey, I bet Luther knows the best place to break out of school."

Luther's grin faltered. "Nope."

"*No?*"

"Well, not exactly." He shifted his coils. "But Geronimo did mention a hole someplace over near the lunchroom where he escaped a couple times."

"There you go," said Fuzzy. "We hit the cafeteria and work it out from there."

His stomach flip-flopped, but he pasted a brave expression on his face. Leading field trips was harder than he'd thought. Still, would Stuart Little cringe from a minor challenge like this? Would Despereaux?

Fuzzy drew himself up. If his heroes could do it, then so could he.

"Follow me, guys!" He marched back up the plank. Amazingly enough, they all followed him.

Along through the crawl space they went. When the group reached a spot above where a corridor should be, Fuzzy stopped and pried up a ceiling tile. Luther peered through the crack beside him. The floor looked a long, long way down.

"Only one of us can fly, ace," hissed the snake.

"And before you ask," squawked Sassafras, "this is not Air Parakeet. I'm not carrying anyone."

Fuzzy forced a chuckle. "So we, uh, find another way."

"Is our trip leader having a problem?" asked Cinnabun.

"Nope. No problem here."

Squeezing his head and part of his body through the gap, Luther scoped out the hallway below.

"Anything?" asked Fuzzy.

"Pull me up," came the boa's muffled voice.

"Pull you up?" said Sassafras. "I thought you were pure muscle."

"I am," said Luther, "but this boa don't go in reverse."

The other three animals gripped his coils and hauled on Luther's body. After a few tugs, they'd pulled him far enough back that he could manage the rest.

"Supply closet next door." Luther jerked his head to the right. "Bound to be plenty of stuff to climb down."

"Maybe even some pink pens with daisies on them!" said Cinnabun.

"Uh, yeah," said Fuzzy. "Maybe. Let's go!"

Through trial and error, they found a ceiling tile that opened into the supply closet. One by one, they climbed, slithered, or flew down to the floor. Shelves stacked with paper, pens, old textbooks, and random school supplies loomed over them like bullies surrounding an easy mark. The room was dim. The stink of ink was strong.

Striding over to the door, Fuzzy gave it a shove. Nothing. He might as well have pushed a rhino.

"Another little detail?" asked Cinnabun. "Are we having fun figuring it out?"

He cleared his throat. "Just a, er, minor setback. We need to get out of this room, so . . ." Scanning the walls, Fuzzy spotted a heating vent by the baseboard. "There! We, um, remove the grate and crawl through that little passage behind it."

Sassafras and Cinnabun exchanged a look. "And how, exactly, do we remove it?" asked the bunny.

Fuzzy slipped his claws between the metal slats and tugged. The plate didn't budge.

"Just a thought," said Luther, "but did you know I can turn doorknobs using only my brawny bod?"

"Great idea!" Fuzzy laughed nervously. "Let's do that."

He and the other two pets watched as the boa slithered back up the shelf closest to the exit, unlocked the doorknob button with his mouth, and looped a coil over the knob.

"This part's a bit tricky," said Luther. "I could use a hand, so to speak."

"What do you need?" asked Fuzzy.

"When I turn this knob, you open the door."

Fuzzy nodded. "I'm on it."

Anchoring his tail to the shelf, Luther twisted the knob and leaned away from the door. It opened just an inch, but that was enough for Fuzzy to get a grip on the edge of the wood.

He braced his feet, then yanked with all his might, just as the boa said, "Easy, now. You don't wanna—"

The door popped open, stretching the snake to his limit. "Gack!" Luther made a strangled noise.

The shelf tilted alarmingly.

Cinnabun and Sassafras leaped back as a heavy rain of erasers, binders, pencils, and boa came pelting down onto Fuzzy. It felt like an avalanche had landed, squashing him like a spider.

He couldn't move. He couldn't breathe.

For a long, long moment, everything was dark and still. Was this the afterlife? Fuzzy felt a bitter rush of regret. How could he have died before he even had his first adventure? This was *so* not fair.

"Brother Fuzzy?" Cinnabun's voice sounded just like an angel's.

Go to the light, he thought. *But all I can see is darkness.*

"Did he croak over?" asked Sassafras. "If he did, I want his ball."

Then, with a groan, a heavy weight shifted off him and slithered to one side. "Wow," said Luther. "That was one crazy ride."

Fuzzy sucked in a breath. He felt dizzy. His back hurt, and he still couldn't see anything.

"Help me dig him out," said Cinnabun.

Scrabbling sounds, then someone lifted a binder out of the way, and he could see again. Apparently, the afterlife would have to wait.

Fuzzy blinked. "Did I open the door?"

"And a few of my vertebrae," said Luther, twisting to look at his back.

"Still want to visit that market?" asked Sassafras.

Staggering to his feet and shaking himself, Fuzzy said, "Just try and stop me."

"No need," said the parakeet. "You almost stopped yourself."

Fuzzy looked around. A classroom's worth of school supplies had fallen with Luther, turning the closet into a disaster area. But the door hung open about six inches, and a lighted hallway beckoned beyond it.

"Hello, adventure," said Fuzzy. He brushed himself off and stepped through the doorway. "Who's with me?"

The other pets followed as he headed down the corridor. A grin stole across Fuzzy's face. Yes, they'd encountered challenges, but they'd met them. He was finally going on a field trip with his friends. Nothing could stop him now!

That delicious feeling lasted right up until they turned the corner to enter the lunchroom and nearly ran into a tall man in brown coveralls with a mop.

"What, in the ever-lovin' blue blazes," said Darius the janitor, "is going on here?"

CHAPTER 7

Jailbreak Blues

It felt like prison. Or at least the way Fuzzy imagined prison felt, based on the TV shows he'd seen at students' houses. Mr. Darius was attaching a wire mesh top to his cage—the cage that had always been open so that kids could pick him up and cuddle.

His freedom was gone—just like that.

"It's all a mistake," Fuzzy squeaked, racing about. "You got the wrong rodent!"

"Sorry, little buddy," said the janitor. "Can't have you getting lost and starving to death, or munched by a mean old cat."

Fuzzy's heartbeat did a drum roll. He gripped the cage bars. "Not fair!"

But the custodian made no reply.

After the Supply Closet Incident, Mr. Darius and the teachers beefed up security measures for the classroom pets. For a full week, Fuzzy heard nothing from his friends.

Not that he particularly wanted to.

He knew they must blame him for getting caught. Sassafras had screeched as much when the janitor was chasing her around the hallway. And she wasn't alone. Fuzzy blamed himself too.

For days, he sulked in his cage, not even nibbling on his favorite chew toy, a stuffed tiger. How could he have been so cocky? He knew nothing about planning a field trip—less than nothing. Yet he led his friends blindly into trouble, and now security was so tight, they might never escape again.

Miss Wills began to worry. She and her students tried to tempt Fuzzy with parsley, pumpkin, and other special foods that he rarely got to eat. They coddled him, carried him around on a pillow, and played with him.

And slowly, slowly, as the days passed, Fuzzy's natural optimism began to seep back. Finally, he sat down in his igloo and gave himself a talking-to. So he'd made a mistake. Big deal. Everybody made mistakes. The point was, what did you learn from them?

During science class, while the kids studied guinea pig anatomy (a ticklish subject), Fuzzy considered how to do things better next time.

If the other pets gave him a next time.

Later, when Loud Brandon practiced his read-aloud skills by the cage, Fuzzy listened attentively. But he couldn't help running over the Supply Closet Incident in his mind, wondering what went wrong.

Just as Brandon reached an exciting part of *Bud, Not Buddy*, the answer came to Fuzzy. "That's it!" he chirped.

The boy's face lit up. "Hey, Miss Wills! Fuzzy likes my reading."

"Of course," said the teacher. "He's got good taste."

What Fuzzy had was a good idea. He and the other pets had been caught because they were walking around in plain sight. What they needed to find was a sneaky way out of school, some trick so they wouldn't be spotted.

Disguises, maybe? Or perhaps they could hide inside something, like a baby kangaroo hid in a pouch? He purred to himself. This idea held promise!

Now that he had a direction, Fuzzy chafed against his captivity. He wanted to see the other pets and discuss his ideas. What had they been up to all week? Were they holding club meetings without him, or were they in lockdown too? He had to find out.

After school that day, Fuzzy decided the time had come to escape. He put the ball and blocks in position, and climbed up on top of them. Then he pushed against the wire mesh ceiling with his forepaws. It held.

Turning around, he braced his feet, set his shoulders against the cage top, and drove upward with all his might. The wire gave a little, forming a perfect impression of Fuzzy's shoulders.

But it didn't break.

"Aw, cat doodies!" he moaned. "There's gotta be a way out."

Just then, a rustling and clattering came from somewhere up above. Scanning the classroom ceiling, Fuzzy noticed one of the tiles was moving. Had a squirrel or rat broken into school somehow?

The panel slid aside, and a familiar face peeked out. "Sassafras!"

"Ta-da!" squawked the parakeet. She gazed down at him. "We've got a club meeting today. Why are you still in that cage?"

"I'm working on my suntan," he said.

"Huh?"

"They, uh, beefed up my security," said Fuzzy, painfully aware that his botched field trip had caused the change. "Help a rodent out?"

Nudging the ceiling tile aside, Sassafras dropped through the hole, unfurled her wings, and glided to the cage top. "And she sticks the landing!" she crowed.

"Don't you always?" said Fuzzy. "Come on, get me out of here."

Strutting along the wire mesh, the parakeet cocked her head this way and that, studying it closely. "Mm-hmm," she said, and, "interesting."

"What?"

"Your cage has a top on it now."

Fuzzy rolled his eyes. "Really? I hadn't noticed."

"Oh yeah," said Sassafras. "That's definitely a top."

He ground his teeth. "So how do we get it off? I tried pushing."

Nodding wisely, the parakeet said, "Ah, that explains the Fuzzy-shaped lump in the wire."

"Thank you, Sherlock Holmes," said Fuzzy. "Do you see any weak spots? Any way to punch a hole in this thing?"

Sassafras tilted her head back and closed one eye, considering. "Mm, I think they'd notice a hole, and then they'd tighten security even more."

"Great," said Fuzzy. "Just great." He inspected the edge where the cage top met the sides. It was flush, all the way around. No gaps. But then he noticed something.

"Hey, check this out," he said, rattling the top. "The only things holding this in place are these little wire bits tying it to the sides. If we could take them off somehow . . ."

"Then we could get you out," said Sassafras. She puffed up her chest. "I always have the most brilliant ideas."

"Always," said Fuzzy. He examined one of the ties. "But look, it's all twisted together." Fuzzy tried to undo the wire, but his paws couldn't find a grip.

"Here, allow *moi*," said the bird. Leaning over, she took the twisted ends in her beak and rotated her head. "Did that do it?"

"Not quite," said Fuzzy. "Once more."

Sassafras repeated the action, and this time she separated the wire ends far enough for Fuzzy to untwist them the rest of the way. They repeated the process for two more ties.

"Try it now," said the parakeet.

Fuzzy again braced his shoulders and pushed on the top. This time, it moved, but not quite enough for him to squeeze through a gap. Then he saw the reason.

"Um, this might be easier if you got off the cage," he said.

"Oh." Sassafras looked down at him. "Yeah."

She spread her wings and glided to the floor.

With a push and a wriggle, Fuzzy opened a gap at the corner of his cage and squeezed his way through it. "Hey, I'm free!" he squeaked, raising his paws in victory. Then he lost his balance and tumbled to the floor, landing with a thump.

Whappity-whoppity.

"Oof!"

"If you're done with your acrobatics," said Sassafras, "can we go now?"

As the pair crept through the crawl space above the classrooms, Sassafras updated Fuzzy on the other pets.

"Everyone who went on the field trip got tighter security," she said, ducking under a duct. "Luther was the first to break out. That old escape artist freed me and Cinnabun yesterday."

Fuzzy felt a little hurt that the boa hadn't visited him already, but he swallowed his disappointment. "Are they pretty mad at me?" he asked.

"I don't know about them," said the parakeet, "but I don't blame you."

"You don't?"

She flapped a wing. "Nah, it was just bad luck. Plus, I loved it when Luther stretched like a bungee cord. *Boing!*"

By the time they reached the clubhouse, the whole gang had gathered. Luther and Igor were having a spirited discussion, Mistletoe and Cinnabun were nibbling a snack bar, and Marta was napping. Everyone but the tortoise looked up when Fuzzy and Sassafras entered.

"At last," said Igor. "Mr. Big Shot decided to join us."

Fuzzy gave an embarrassed smile. "I, uh, needed help with my jailbreak. Good to see you guys."

Daintily brushing crumbs from her downy fur, Cinnabun said, "Now that all of y'all are here, let's begin, shall we?" She hopped up onto the presidential podium and rapped her gavel.

"So graceful." Mistletoe sighed.

"Whazza?" mumbled Marta, waking up.

The bunny gazed around the group. "This meeting of the Class Pets Club is now called to order. Any old business to discuss?"

Igor raised a lazy paw. "Yes, when Mistletoe gets us snacks, could she pick something other than PowerBars?"

"What's wrong with PowerBars?" asked Marta.

The iguana grimaced. "They taste like sawdust, and they don't work."

"How do you mean?" asked Sassafras.

"I've been eating them constantly, but I'm not any stronger."

Cinnabun nodded. "Duly noted, Brother Igor. All in favor?" Nearly every paw went up. "Sister Mistletoe, would you see about getting some more variety into our snacks?"

"For you?" said the mouse. "Anything."

Fuzzy just managed to keep from rolling his eyes. Snacks could wait. It was time to find out where he stood. He raised a paw.

"Yes, Brother Fuzzy?" said Cinnabun.

"I, uh, think we should take another field trip," he said.

The other pets muttered to one another, and Luther shot him a cold look. Not very promising.

Cinnabun's expression was gently reproachful. "Now, you know as well as I do that a future event would fall under new business."

"Oh," said Fuzzy. "So when can we talk about it?"

"Right after old business," said the bunny. She glanced around the room. "Any more old business?"

Luther said, "Yeah, this farmers' market trip was poorly planned, and it gave me a sprain in the membrane. I vote we don't do that again anytime soon."

"Future actions are new business," Cinnabun reminded him.

"Look, I'm really sorry about how it turned out,"

said Fuzzy, ignoring her. "But I learned a lot. We'll do it better next time."

"Ain't gonna be a next time," said the boa, sticking out his forked tongue.

Wagging a paw, Cinnabun said, "Ah-ah-ah. 'Next time' also comes under the heading of new business. Gentlemen, if we don't follow the rules of order, we're nothing but anarchists."

"What's . . . andy-kissed?" asked Sassafras, grooming her wing.

"Someone who doesn't follow rules," said the bunny. "And I'm sure none of you lovely pets are that kind of animal."

Not wanting to disappoint their president, the others shook their heads.

Fuzzy felt his temperature rise a few degrees. "Can I at least say what I learned from what went wrong?"

Cinnabun cocked her head, considering. "That does relate to old business, so I suppose that's allowed."

He spread his paws. "Look, I'm sorry that I sprained your membrane, Luther, and I'm sorry we got caught. But I learned two things from it. First—"

"A boa is not a rubber band?" said Luther.

"We need to have a solid plan before we go, and everyone should contribute to it," said Fuzzy.

"You got that right," said the boa.

"And second, if we want our plan to succeed we need to find a way to sneak out without being seen."

Marta nodded. "Very sensible."

"Works for me," said Sassafras, shifting from foot to foot. "Now can we stop talking and do something? I'm getting bored."

"One moment, please," said Cinnabun. "Any more old business?"

Everyone shook their heads.

"On to new business," she said. "Brother Luther, do you still want to ban all future trips, even though Brother Fuzzy has apologized and offered ideas for improvement?"

All eyes turned to the boa. Fuzzy took a deep breath. Luther held his future in his hands (or whatever passed for hands with snakes). The boa had the power to end all of Fuzzy's dreams of adventure, right on the spot.

What would he do?

CHAPTER 8

Meet the Dinos

The snake's mouth twisted. He looked from Fuzzy to the other pets, eyes narrowed. At long last, he sighed. "I withdraw my suggestion," he said.

Fuzzy gasped, "Thank you!" All the air seemed to whoosh out of him as he relaxed. The future looked bright again.

"Under one condition," said Luther.

"Anything."

"There will be no hanging from, climbing on, or painful stretching of this beautiful, snaky bod."

Fuzzy raised a paw. "I solemnly swear."

"All right then," said the boa.

"Let's continue," said Cinnabun, after sneaking a quick nibble of the presidential podium. "Brother Fuzzy, do you know where we might go, if we do try another field trip?"

Fuzzy chuckled nervously and studied his paws. He hadn't thought quite that far ahead. "Uh, no," he said. "But I'll come up with something soon."

"Peachy keen," said the bunny. "Let's table this discussion until our next meeting. But now *I* have some new business."

Mistletoe wriggled. "Can't wait!"

Cinnabun clapped her paws together. "As your president, I think what this group needs is some team spirit."

"And better snacks," muttered Igor.

"We need to have some fun-fun-fun together," the bunny continued. "And what could be jollier than a good old-fashioned sing-along?"

Fuzzy could think of several things jollier, including a bad case of bumblefoot. But since Cinnabun had backed him with the first field trip, he tried to keep an open mind. It was hard work.

"This is a neato-repeato song," squealed the bunny. "It's neato, and you repeato after me. Ready? Here we go! Itsy bitsy."

"Itsy bitsy," the pets echoed.

"Teeny weeny," sang Cinnabun.

"Teeny weeny."

"Froggy woggy."

"Froggy woggy."

"Loves linguini."

"Loves linguini?"

It went downhill from there. By the time Cinnabun had led them through nine more verses about the itsy-bitsy froggy woggy and followed that up with "Boom-Chicka-Smooch" and a song about the cutest bunny in the world, Fuzzy was ready to hork up his hay.

He left the meeting feeling queasy but hopeful. If he could think of a really exciting field trip, he might win the other pets over. And if he did that, maybe then they'd elect him president sometime before Cinnabun killed them all with terminal cuteness.

A rodent could always hope.

The next day, Fuzzy paid close attention to Miss Wills and the kids. Not only was it part of his job as class pet, but he was also seeking inspiration. Humans were pretty smart creatures, on the whole. Maybe somebody would mention the perfect place for a field trip.

Fuzzy learned lots of new vocabulary words (like *saunter* and *feeble*). He explored Roman numerals and heard all about the scientific method. But not once did anyone mention the ideal place for a bunch of pets to visit.

That Friday, he went home with Maya, the girl with tiny braids. (She was the top student of the week, and top students got pet-sitting honors.) All through the weekend, Fuzzy watched her big family, their scary cats, and their TV shows (yay, SpongeBob!).

Once, her little brother mentioned some place called Disney World, which sounded like a fun place to visit. Fuzzy's ears perked up and a shiver of excitement rippled through him. But when Maya's mom complained that it was a two-day drive away, he quickly lost interest.

Back in class on Monday, Fuzzy was getting worried. Everything depended on his picking the perfect spot for a field trip, and he had to think of it by Wednesday, before the next Class Pets Club meeting. Time was running short. He knew his fellow pets well enough to know they wouldn't give him any more chances if he blew this one.

Then, on Tuesday morning, Fuzzy heard some words that made him smile.

"Boys and girls," said Miss Wills. "Have you ever wanted to learn more about dinosaurs?" Many hands went up. "Would you like to meet extinct animals like the mastodon, Tasmanian tiger, and giant lemur?"

"Yeah!" the students cried.

"Me too!" squeaked Fuzzy.

"Well, next week you'll have your chance," said the teacher. "Because next week we'll be going on our first field trip of the year to . . . drum roll, please!"

Faces shining, the kids pounded their thighs with their palms.

"The natural history museum!" Miss Wills cried.

Cheers erupted. Fuzzy jumped up and down with a *wheek, wheek!* He hadn't known about the place before, but he recognized the perfect field trip location when he heard it. Dinosaurs? Animals that no one living had ever seen?

The gang was going to flip for this idea.

Once things had settled down, the teacher passed out permission slips and explained more about the outing. "We'll leave right after recess and be gone most of the day," she said.

"What about lunch?" asked Connor, a skinny boy who was always snacking.

"We'll bring sack lunches and hold a picnic in the museum courtyard," said Miss Wills. "Everyone should take their book bags along."

"Do our parents have to drive us?" whined Zoey-with-the-braces. "'Cause mine both have to work."

"No worries," said Miss Wills. "We'll be taking a bus."

"This is awesome!" cried Loud Brandon. "I love dinosaurs!"

The teacher laughed. "You're not alone, Brandon."

Fuzzy couldn't wait to share this news with his fellow pets. He trotted up and down the cage, *wheek*ing for all he was worth.

"Hey, Fuzzy wants to go too," said Heavy-Handed Jake. "Can we bring him along? Please?"

The teacher shook her head. "Sorry, but the museum doesn't allow animals."

"No fair!"

"What about the dinosaurs and giant lemurs?" said Fuzzy. "They're animals."

Miss Wills stuck a finger between the cage bars and stroked his back. "I know you don't like it, boy. Me neither, but rules are rules."

Fuzzy scowled. He was going to break those rules like an anarchist, but he and the other pets would have to be very careful not to get caught. *This calls for a lot of planning,* he thought.

No way could he hold out until tomorrow's meeting to share the big news. Fuzzy just had to tell someone *now*. After school, he waited for Darius Poole to come clean the room. The tall janitor found him pacing up and down, bursting with excitement.

"Hey, little buddy," called Mr. Darius. "Couldn't wait to see me, eh?" Striding up to the cage on his long legs, he dug a couple of grapes from his breast pocket.

As the man bent down to share the treat, Fuzzy suddenly noticed that the wires he and Sassafras had undone for his escape were still dangling open. Suffering mange mites! Miss Wills hadn't noticed, but would Mr. Darius?

If Mr. Darius re-twisted the ties, Fuzzy would be trapped again until someone helped him.

"Got a little treat for you, pal," said the janitor.

"Oh boy, oh boy, oh boy!" squeaked Fuzzy, turning in circles. He hoped his actions would distract the man.

"Wow, you must love grapes," said Mr. Darius. "Next time I'll bring more." He watched with a bittersweet smile as Fuzzy stuffed them into his cheeks. "Wish my life was like yours. You don't know anything about money troubles or ex-wives. Must be sweet, just eating, playing, and being petted all day."

Fuzzy felt torn. He knew he should listen to his friend's woes, but he really didn't want Mr. Darius to spot the dangling wires. Slowly-slowly, with his eyes on the janitor, he sidled over into the area where the ties were still intact.

Mr. Darius shook his head ruefully. "You'd think that someone who used to love you would at least act sort of friendly after you split up."

Fuzzy listened, wearing his saddest expression. He knew that it helped his humans to talk to him when they were upset. And he hoped Mr. Darius would watch him, not the cage.

When the janitor glanced over, he broke into a chuckle. "Don't look so worried, little buddy. It'll all work out eventually."

He gave the cage a pat and then cocked his head. Fuzzy's heartbeat thudded in his ears. This was it. Mr. Darius had spotted the undone wires and would tighten them so tightly that Fuzzy would never escape again.

But all the big man said was, "Thanks for listening, buddy." He turned away to empty the wastebaskets, and Fuzzy collapsed in relief.

As the door locked behind the janitor, Fuzzy blew out a gusty sigh. All this intrigue was hard on a rodent's nerves. Still, Fuzzy scrambled to his feet, pushed his blocks and ball together, and made his escape. Trotting along through the warm crawl space, he decided to pay Mistletoe a visit. She was just the pet to share his big news with.

When he reached Room 3-A, Fuzzy nudged a ceiling tile aside and peeked down at the room below. All was quiet. "Mistletoe!" he called. "Are you awake?"

"Wh-who's there?" came the mouse's voice. "Is it a ghost?"

"It's me, Fuzzy."

"I don't see anybody. How do I know you're not a ghost pretending to be Fuzzy?"

He shook his head. Mistletoe was predictably Mistletoe. He climbed down onto the top of a high cabinet and began making his way toward the mouse's cage.

"I have . . . some great news," he said, edging carefully around bins of art supplies.

Eyes wide, Mistletoe poked her head from her cage. "Oh, there you are. What's up? Did the teachers leave leftovers in their break room again?"

Fuzzy leaped from the cabinet onto a high work-table. "Even better. I know where we're going on our next field trip." He told her all about the natural history museum and its wonders.

Mistletoe's mouth dropped open in amazement. But then, her eyebrows drew together. "Are you sure none of these big animals are still alive?"

"Dead as leaves in the fall," said Fuzzy.

She nibbled her lip. "And there's nothing there that likes to eat mice?"

"Nothing at all."

"Whoopee!" squeaked Mistletoe. "We're going on a field trip!"

CHAPTER 9

To Go, or Not to Go?

At the next day's meeting, the clubhouse buzzed with questions and concerns.

"How do we get there without being seen?" asked Marta.

"How do we keep anyone from noticing that we're gone?" asked Sassafras.

"Are you out of your piggy little mind?" asked Igor.

Fuzzy held up his paws. "These are things we can work out together. But first, what about our destination?" He scanned his fellow pets' faces. "Is it cool enough for a field trip?"

Cinnabun wiggled her nose, considering. "Well, this museum doesn't sound like it has any daisies or unicorns."

"Flowers, maybe," said Fuzzy. "Unicorns? I don't know."

"Is it pretty?" she asked.

"Who cares if it's pretty?" said Sassafras. "There's dinosaurs. I think I might be related to one of them." She puffed out her chest.

"You might be related to an avalanche too," sneered Igor.

"Why's that?" asked Sassafras.

"You've got rocks in your head."

"Really?" asked Mistletoe.

Sassafras glowered at Igor. "Says the lizard with a face like five miles of gravel road."

The iguana snarled, the parakeet bristled, and Cinnabun rapped her gavel. "Now, now, friends. Let's not fly off the handle. We're trying to decide whether the club will take this field trip, not hold an insult competition."

"Which I would totally win," drawled Igor.

"In your dreams," said Sassafras.

"Let's hear the pros and cons before we vote," said the bunny. "Who'd like to start us off with some pros?"

"It's an exciting place with lots of cool exhibits to see," said Fuzzy.

"It'll get us out of school for a while," said Luther, winding around the cat sculpture.

"Plus, did I mention dinosaurs?" squawked Sassafras.

Cinnabun thanked them with a smile. "And the cons?"

"It sounds far away," said Marta the tortoise.

"It might be scary," said Mistletoe.

Igor scowled. "We'd have to leave the school and everything we know behind."

"Only for a half day," Fuzzy said. "Some of your naps last that long."

The iguana's scowl deepened. "Listen, pellet brain—"

Cinnabun held up a calming paw. "Ah-ah-ah, gentlemen. No need to get personal. Now I think we're about ready to take a vote."

Fuzzy looked around. He could tell that the club was dividing along the usual lines. If he didn't act now, before they voted, the pets would very likely reject his idea.

And that might mean the end of adventures.

He got a sinking feeling in his belly.

It was time for a silver-tongued speaker to step up. But since there were no silver-tongued speakers around, Fuzzy would have to do. Wading into the middle of the group, he rose onto his hind paws and lifted his arms for quiet.

"Four square and seven years ago," he said, "our ancestors came to this school to seek out new life and new civilizations, to boldly go where—"

"Didn't I hear that on a TV show?" squawked Sassafras.

Fuzzy's ears burned. "Uh, I have a dream that one day, in the halls of Leo Gumpus, the sons of reptiles and the sons of mammals will—"

"What are you blabbering about?" said Igor.

"I, um . . ." Fuzzy's face fell. This speaking thing was harder than it seemed.

He gulped. "Look, here's what I wanted to say. Before you make up your mind, remember this. As pets, we've made the ultimate sacrifice."

Sassafras preened her wing feathers. "Our lives?"

Fuzzy shook his head. "Our freedom. We've sacrificed our freedom for regular meals and a comfy place to live."

"Don't forget snuggles," said Cinnabun. "Love those snugglies."

"Snuggles too," he agreed. "We spend most of our lives caged up, while humans come and go as they please, seeing the whole wide world. They have adventures wherever and whenever they want. Don't you wish you could too?"

He searched the other pets' faces. Some of them were nodding; others looked thoughtful.

"This is a chance to taste our freedom," said Fuzzy. "To go where we please, to experience new things and new places." He put a paw to his chest. "This isn't about us, though."

"It's not?" asked Mistletoe, thoroughly confused.

He stared past their clubhouse, off into a misty future. "When we go out there as free animals, we're not just doing it for ourselves. We're doing it for all the pets everywhere who long for freedom—for their babies, and their babies' babies."

"Yeah, baby," said Luther.

"So when you cast your vote, do it for yourself, yes, but do it for freedom," said Fuzzy. "And do it . . . for all the class pets yet to come." Recovering himself, he found that his eyes were misty and his throat tight. "Thank you."

Fuzzy stepped out of the circle and sat down.

"That was so inspiring," murmured Mistletoe, patting his shoulder. "The parts I understood, anyway."

Glancing at the other pets, Fuzzy wondered whether his speech would be enough. His shoulders tensed.

"Members of the Class Pets Club, it is time to vote on this motion," said Cinnabun solemnly. "All in favor of taking this field trip?"

Fuzzy raised his paw. Sassafras lifted a wing.

Biting his lip, Fuzzy watched as one by one, all the other pets voted in favor of the field trip—all but Igor. To Fuzzy's questioning look, the iguana said, "Hey, someone's got to keep it real. This is a nutty idea."

"The motion is carried!" Cinnabun rapped her gavel on *The Complete Works of William Shakespeare*. "Whether it has unicorns or not, we are going to the museum."

A rush of relief flooded through Fuzzy, and his knees went rubbery.

"Fabulous!" squawked Sassafras. "Can't wait to meet my relatives."

Marta and Mistletoe congratulated Fuzzy, while Luther shot him a wink. "Nice job, Fuzzarino."

He accepted their congratulations. When things simmered down, Fuzzy turned to the group. "Igor's right."

"I am?" said Igor.

"This is a nutty idea, but sometimes in life you've got to get a little bit crazy. And now we have to combine our craziness. This trip will only work if we all put our heads together."

Mistletoe butted her noggin up against Marta's.

"Uh, figure of speech," said Fuzzy.

The mouse blinked twice. "I knew that."

"There's a lot to work out," said Fuzzy. "And we'd better start working."

Cinnabun peered over the podium. "First things first," she said. "When were you thinking we might visit this lovely museum?"

"When the students go, of course," said Fuzzy.

"But won't it take us forever to walk there?" asked Marta.

He grinned. "Who said anything about walking?"

"But how else—" Marta began. A light dawned in her eyes. "You mentioned the students will be riding a bus?"

"That's right. And we'll be on that bus too."

Mistletoe frowned. "What do you mean?"

"We'll be stowaways."

Luther scratched his head against the cat statue. "And how exactly will that happen?"

"Well . . ." Fuzzy spread his paws. "That's the first thing we need to figure out."

The pets plotted and planned into the early evening, suggesting and rejecting ideas right and left.

"We could disguise ourselves as students," said Mistletoe.

"Nah," said the rest of the group.

"We're much too short," said Cinnabun gently. "They'd spot it in a second."

The mouse slumped, picking at the seam of a pillow.

Fuzzy perked up. "Ooh, we could dig a tunnel out to the bus!"

"Nah," said the rest of the group.

"Too much work," said Igor. "Plus, how do we get from the hole to the bus without being seen?"

"And how do we know which direction to dig, once we're underground?" said Luther.

Fuzzy rubbed his jaw. "Good point." He stood, stretched, and scratched himself. Figuring out a plan was hard work, but he was glad they were doing it together.

At long last, when Marta and Igor were both yawning, they decided to call it a night. Of course, the pets still had to sing a couple of cutesy songs ("Happy Happy Boogaloo" and "Sweetie-Pie Pie") before President Cinnabun would let them go. Fuzzy didn't think it was possible, but her songs actually seemed to be getting worse.

Still, she'd supported his trip. So he gritted his teeth and pretended to sing along.

Cinnabun set their next meeting for Monday. Several key issues still needed resolving, but the field trip was one week away, and Fuzzy had to trust that everything would work out.

But later that night, as he settled down in his bed of pine shavings, Fuzzy's doubts returned full force:

Am I smart enough to lead this trip?

Can we really get away with it?

And how in the world will we get onto that bus?

He tossed and turned, but Fuzzy had no answers.

CHAPTER 10

A Doggy Day

By the time the weekend rolled around, Fuzzy felt like one of those spring-loaded snakes in a joke box—full of tension and ready to explode. Progress was glacially slow. If he didn't figure things out by Monday's meeting, Cinnabun would pull the plug on this trip for sure.

And that would be that. No more adventures. Ever.

So, no pressure there.

Given all that, it was hard not to resent having to visit Spiky Diego's house for the weekend. But the boy had won top honors that week, and being pet-sat by the best student was part of a class pet's job. Fuzzy tried not to fret as Miss Wills gave him a final cuddle and low-ered him into the pet carrier.

"Be good, little guy," she told him. "And Diego, call me anytime with questions."

"Don't worry, Miss Wills," said Spiky Diego. "I've had lots of pets. We'll be fine."

Fuzzy hoped so. But more than that, he hoped the weekend at the boy's house would inspire him. He needed inspiration.

Desperately.

His first introduction to Diego's family was less than promising. The boy carried him through the door into what seemed like a madhouse. Three little girls ran past, screaming like their hair was on fire. An older girl paced with a finger jammed in one ear, bellowing into her cell phone. And a deep, booming *WOOF-WOOF-WOOF!* put all the other noisemakers to shame.

"Welcome to Casa Garcia," said Spiky Diego. "We're gonna have some fun this weekend."

Fuzzy doubted it very much.

The first order of business: meeting the Barker-in-

Chief. Diego set the cage down, and an enormous shape immediately loomed over it, blotting out all light in the room. Fuzzy cowered in a corner.

"Fuzzy, this is Blue," said the boy.

A gust of horrendous doggy breath swept through the carrier as the monster pressed its nose to the wire. A gale-force *WOOF!* blew back Fuzzy's hair. He peeked out from behind his paws to see a dog as big as a pony, with blue-gray fur and a long, mournful face.

"You be good to Fuzzy," said Diego. "He's our guest."

Fuzzy wondered if Blue understood the difference between *guest* and *snack*. He trembled a little, and a squeak may have escaped his lips.

Diego's hands entered the cage and lifted out a terrified Fuzzy. The boy held him softly, with one hand under his haunches and one around his torso. But the gentle handling did nothing to ease Fuzzy's terror.

"Get me out of here!" he squealed.

"There's nothing to be afraid of," said Spiky Diego. "Blue, this is Fuzzy. Say hello—nicely." He held Fuzzy at eye level to a head the size of a sphinx.

"H-h-hi there," said Fuzzy.

Blue's nose took up Fuzzy's whole field of vision. It made a snorfling sound as the dog sniffed him thoroughly.

Fuzzy braced himself. Would he be eaten alive, or just inhaled?

"WELCOME, LITTLE ONE," boomed Blue. A tongue as broad as a carpet gave him a massive lick.

"Uh, th-thanks," Fuzzy stuttered. Totally drenched, he tried not to show how much he hated smelling like a dog's breakfast. "N-nice place you have here."

"MY HOME," the dog thundered. "MY RULES."

"Whatever you say, big guy."

Then the front door opened. With another deafening bark, Blue galloped to greet the visitor.

"Doesn't he have a volume control?" Fuzzy muttered.

When Diego turned, Fuzzy saw that the newcomer was a smiling woman lugging a huge pink purse. She had the same sparkly dark eyes and full cheeks as the boy.

"Mom, look!" said Spiky Diego. "I made the best grades this week, so I got to bring Fuzzy home."

"The more, the merrier," said Diego's mom, giving her boy a kiss. When she did, a muffled yipping came from her purse. "Oh, I almost forgot about Lola."

She unzipped the bag and a dog's head poked out. But what a dog. It was nearly hairless, with huge pop-eyes and ears like a bat. Not much bigger than Fuzzy, this dog was the opposite of Blue in every way.

"Who are you?" the dog snapped. "What are you doing here? Why have you come? You can't have any of my food—no way, buster! So back off!"

Fuzzy recoiled. "I don't want your food. I'm Fuzzy, and I'm only here for the weekend."

"You just keep that in mind, bucko!" the little dog yipped. "Don't get comfortable, and don't get any ideas about moving in. *I'm* the cute one here!"

"Chill, Lola," said Diego. He turned his body, so Fuzzy and the snippety dog weren't face-to-face anymore. "She's real nice," he confided, "once you get to know her."

But Fuzzy wasn't listening. He'd just been struck speechless by a big idea.

If Diego's mom carried Lola around in a bag, why couldn't other animals travel that way—say, for example, the Class Pets Club? Fuzzy and his friends were small enough to fit into book bags. What if they sneaked into the fifth graders' bags to get on and off the bus?

"Brilliant!" squeaked Fuzzy, wriggling in Diego's hands. "Thanks, Lola!"

Mrs. Garcia must have released her, because the little dog trotted around Spiky Diego, yipping, "What are you thanking me for? Don't thank me, you tailless rat. I'm not on your side! You're—"

"I'm a guinea pig, actually," said Fuzzy.

Diego's mom scooped up the dog in one hand. "Enough, *pequeña*," she said. "You give me a headache."

Lola's rant continued undiminished as Mrs. Garcia carried her off. Blue added a few more *WOOF*s. And as someone unseen began to practice electric guitar, the three little girls came squealing up to the big dog, trying to ride him like a horse.

"Welcome to my world," Spiky Diego told Fuzzy.

As it turned out, the shouting, barking, music playing, and TV's blare were almost constant. But Diego's people and dogs didn't seem mad at one another, just full of energy. The volume didn't let up for meals, or anything, really. Except sleep.

Fuzzy couldn't object too much—he lived in a fifth-grade classroom, after all—but he welcomed the quiet that came at night. All through the weekend he paid close attention to the family, waiting for more inspiration.

But the hours passed, and it never came.

Diego had installed him on a table in the family room, in an open-topped cage that smelled of hamsters. There, Fuzzy was safe from short-tempered Lola, but right on eye level with the gigantic Blue. He hoped the family was feeding the monstrous dog enough. It wouldn't take more than a second for him to lean into the cage and snarf up a guinea pig.

The wide-screen TV was always on, blasting out cartoons, sports, and movies. After a day or so, Fuzzy learned to tune it out. But on his final night with the Garcias, the TV said something that caught his attention.

"Yes, friends," an announcer purred, "it's time for another Channel Five Sunday movie marathon. Today's theme: prison-break movies."

Fuzzy stood bolt upright, banging into the top of the cardboard tube he'd been exploring. Prison-break movies? Very promising indeed. He scuttled out of the tube and gripped his cage bars, watching the screen.

"First up," said the TV man, "that old classic, *The Shawshank Redemption*, followed by *Escape from Alcatraz*, *Papillon*, and the granddaddy of them all, *The Great Escape*."

Normally, Fuzzy didn't care much for movies without animals in them, but this time, he couldn't tear his eyes away.

He stared as the tall man in *The Shawshank Redemption* concealed his escape tunnel with a poster. He gaped as the prisoners in Alcatraz made dummies to act as decoys. He gasped as the inmate in *The Great Escape* tried evading the soldiers on a motorcycle.

Who knew that TV could be so educational?

Long past his bedtime, Fuzzy finally settled down to sleep. And in his dreams, he dreamed of freedom, escape.

And adventures.

CHAPTER 11

Dummying Up

Of course, it was one thing to watch people on TV making bold escape attempts. It was a whole other thing to try making one yourself.

"I still don't get it," Mistletoe said at their Monday Class Pets Club meeting. "Why do we have to make dummies?"

"Because we don't want anyone to notice we're gone," said Fuzzy.

She wrinkled her brow. "And how does that work again?"

Fuzzy tried not to grind his teeth. "You leave the dummy behind in your cage when you go."

"With Mistletoe, who could tell the difference?" drawled the iguana.

Cinnabun frowned. "Now, Brother Igor."

"And if the students see a little Mistletoe-shaped lump in your cage," said Fuzzy, "they'll think you're only sleeping, not gone."

"Oh," said the mouse. "Okay."

Cinnabun frowned. "I worry about my artistic skills."

"Why's that, Missy Miss?" asked Luther.

"I don't think I can make a dummy pretty enough for them to believe it's me."

With a sigh, Fuzzy said, "It doesn't have to be pretty, it just needs to be the same size and shape. Hopefully no one will check too closely."

Discussion was lively. But Fuzzy felt relieved that it was mostly about *how* to work their escape plan, not whether to escape at all. It seemed like the pets had taken his idea and were running with it.

After they'd talked things out, the rest of Monday afternoon was spent raiding classrooms for dummy-making supplies. Room 2-A yielded plenty of paper, sticky tape, and twine. Room 3-C provided a set of paints and brushes just small enough for Sassafras and Fuzzy to drag up to the clubhouse.

"All right, y'all," said Cinnabun when they'd gathered everything. "Who here is artistic?"

"I've always felt like an artist," said Sassafras. "I'm colorful, after all."

"So's a sunflower," said Igor. "That doesn't mean it can paint a picture."

In the end, everyone decided to create his or her own decoy dummy. Most of the pets used crumpled-up paper or cloth for the body, and twine for the tail. Tape held the whole thing together—although in Mistletoe's case, she got as much tape on herself as she did on the decoy.

Sassafras and Fuzzy did their best to paint the dummies the same color as the pets they represented. But Marta's shell was tricky to match, and Luther's body was even harder. Since the snake had no hands to work with, the other pets made his decoy with socks salvaged from the Lost & Found and stuffed with paper.

The boa cocked his head to look at it. "Hmm," he said.

"Something wrong?" asked Marta.

"Not at all," said Luther. "I just never knew I had athletic stripes."

"When it's painted over, the kids will hardly spot the difference," said Fuzzy. He hoped this was true.

When he finally laid down his brush and stretched, their clubhouse looked like an explosion in an artist's studio. Bits of colored paper lay here and there, and paint spatters covered everything, even the presidential podium.

"Looks like rainbow barf," said Igor with a snide chuckle.

"Language," said Cinnabun.

But seven dummies lay in a row, the result of hours of work. Fuzzy, Mistletoe, and Cinnabun had even collected some of their own shed fur to stick onto their decoys, for that realistic touch.

"I do declare," said the bunny, fanning herself, "y'all are the most hardworking pets I ever did see. Give yourselves a round of applause!"

Tired clapping, or in the boa's case, tail tapping, followed the bunny's declaration. But there were grins all around. Fuzzy heaved an exhausted, happy sigh. They'd taken one step closer to their big adventure.

"I'm bringing my dummy back right now to cuddle with," said Mistletoe. "It's so cute!"

Marta held up a calming foot. "Let the paint dry overnight. We shouldn't bring these decoys into our cages until the night before the field trip."

"Why not?" asked the mouse.

"You don't want to give away our plan, do you?"

Mistletoe solemnly shook her head.

The tortoise eyeballed Sassafras and Fuzzy. "And you two better clean off before you go to bed tonight. The humans will wonder why you're rainbow-colored."

Looking down, Fuzzy noticed that he had more paint splashed on him than a Jackson Pollock original. (His fifth graders had just studied the paint splatter guy in their art unit.)

"Good point," he said. "Remember, everyone, keep a low profile tomorrow. We don't want to act like anything is up."

Igor smirked. "If Luther's profile was any lower, he'd be underground."

"Laugh it up, lizard boy." Luther stuck out his tongue. "What I lack in height, I make up for in length."

Cinnabun hopped onto the podium and rapped the gavel—*bap bap bap.* "We'll see y'all tomorrow after school for final preparations. And now, I declare this meeting to be adjourned."

"What's 'adjourned'?" asked Mistletoe.

"We are," said Sassafras. "That means go to your room and get some rest."

The mouse yawned. "I think I'll adjourn all night long."

It wasn't until Fuzzy was halfway back to Room 5-B that he realized Cinnabun hadn't even made them do something disgustingly adorable at that meeting.

"Things," he told himself, "are definitely looking up."

The next morning dawned clear and cool. But Fuzzy didn't notice. He was so sacked out that he didn't wake up until class began.

As he did his morning exercises, Fuzzy reviewed the trip preparations in his mind. Dummies ready? Check. Boarding plan in place? Check. Of course, he had no idea what would happen once they reached the museum. But then, few of the prisoners in those movies he'd watched had more than a vague plan of what to do after they'd escaped.

Like them, Fuzzy would make it up as he went along. The mere idea left him feeling simultaneously exhilarated and paralyzed with fear.

Maybe this, he thought, *is what adventure feels like.*

Just before the school day ended, Miss Wills addressed the students. "Now, remember, the buses arrive during recess tomorrow. We'll come back to the room to collect our bags before we go. And what does everyone need to bring?"

Pig-tailed Sofia's hand shot up. "Our lunches, Miss Wills."

"That's right, Sofia. Now, a couple of you still haven't turned in your signed permission slips. If I don't have them tomorrow, you'll be staying behind."

"But what will we do if we stay behind?" asked Loud Brandon. Fuzzy suspected he was one of those late students.

"Homework in the library with Mrs. Puka," said the teacher. "So if that's not your idea of heaven, I suggest you bring that slip tomorrow morning."

Brandon bit his lip.

Fuzzy hardly noticed. He was thinking about tomorrow's recess. That was when the pets would need to hide in the book bags, because the backpacks wouldn't be available until after class started.

It'd be quick and easy for Fuzzy, since his fifth graders were going on the field trip. Just slip out of the cage and cross the room. *Bim bam boom.*

But what about the pets from other classrooms? How would they manage?

CHAPTER 12

The Not-So-Great Escape

"We have to *what*?" Marta asked, horrified. "And when?" Her head retracted back into her shell.

Fuzzy patted her gently. "It's not so bad. You've got twenty whole minutes to get from your room into a book bag in the closest fifth-grade class."

This was the pets' last meeting before their big adventure, and more than one of them was getting cold feet.

"I'll never make it in time," said Marta, her voice muffled. "And how will I get down from the ceiling? I've never even seen that room before."

"Would someone kindly volunteer to help Sister

Marta?" asked Cinnabun, giving the other club members her melty-eyed look.

Luther spoke up. "I'll do it, Missy Miss. She's right on my way from 3-C."

"Such a gentleman," said the bunny.

"Maybe I shouldn't go," said the tortoise.

"Aw, come on," said Sassafras. "You don't want to miss the sights, do you?"

"Well . . ."

Mistletoe twisted her long tail in her paws. "Um, if Marta's not going, then I'm not."

"She's going, she's going," said Fuzzy. "Aren't you, Marta?"

The tortoise's head emerged from her shell. She mulled it over for a long minute, surveying the other pets with her wise eyes. "I've lived a long time," she said, "longer than any of you."

"Yeah, we get it," said Igor. "You're old."

"Brother Igor," said Cinnabun. "Manners!"

"What? She's not gonna go."

Fuzzy's gut gave a twist. If Marta bailed out, who knew how many more would follow?

Her brow lifted. "Yes, I'm old. And my life has been long and deliberate. But I've never had an adventure like this, and I've never seen a dinosaur."

"Does that mean . . . ?" Fuzzy asked.

"I'm going," said Marta. "With Luther's help. You're never too old for adventure."

A rush of relief warmed Fuzzy's belly. "Okay, Mistletoe," he said. "She's going. Are you in?"

Wide-eyed, the mouse nibbled her tail. "Um, can I ride in your bag?"

"Absolutely," said Fuzzy.

"Then, I'm in."

A warm purr rumbled in his chest.

Cinnabun hopped off the Shakespeare book. "If I might make a teensy-tiny suggestion?" she said.

"Suggest away," said Sassafras. "You're the prez."

"In the interests of togetherness and safety," said Cinnabun, "why don't we all travel in the same class's bags? That way, no one gets separated if something goes wrong."

Mistletoe gasped. "What's going wrong?"

"Nothing," Fuzzy said. "And I think that's . . . an

excellent idea for keeping the club together." He was more than a little surprised to find himself agreeing with Cinnabun on anything.

The other pets nodded.

"Splendid!" said the bunny. "That's settled. Let's travel with Fuzzy's class, since he can guide us down from the ceiling quickly."

"Works for me," said Luther. "I'll still stop by and help Marta with the tricky bits."

The tortoise sent him a grateful smile. "You're a good snake."

The boa smirked. "That's something you don't hear very often."

With a rush, Fuzzy realized that they were finally doing it; they were finally fulfilling his dream, together. As long as nothing went wrong, that is. "Everyone, don't forget your decoy dummy when you leave today," he said. "The plan won't work without it."

Cinnabun surveyed the group. "Now, if there's no more business related to the field trip . . . ?" Everyone shook their heads. "Then I have a delightful new twist for this week's cuteness contest."

"Oh, joy," said Igor, deadpan.

The rabbit reached behind the podium and produced a frilly pink bow the size of a hothouse flower. "When it's your turn to make an adorable expression, be sure to wear the bow. Doesn't it just put the *C* in *cuteness*?"

Or the Y *in* yucky, thought Fuzzy. He gritted his teeth in a forced smile.

"Brother Fuzzy," said Cinnabun, "why don't you start?"

As he accepted the dreaded pink ribbon, Fuzzy had another thought. A year was a long time to suffer while waiting for his chance to be president, and a museum had lots of confusing nooks and crannies.

Wouldn't it be a shame if President Cinnabun got lost in one of them?

When Miss Wills's students arrived the next morning, they were particularly bubbly. Apparently, Fuzzy wasn't the only one excited about the field trip.

"Today's the day," said Maya to Zoey-with-the-braces. "I can't wait."

"Me neither," said Zoey. "I've decided to spend all my time at the dinosaur exhibit. I'm going to be a pale-ontologist when I grow up."

Fuzzy didn't know what that was, but it sounded important. The class's excitement fed his own, and soon he was hopping around the cage, squealing for all he was worth.

Wheek! Wheek!

"Ha!" laughed Heavy-Handed Jake. "Fuzzy wants to go too!"

If you only knew, thought Fuzzy.

Somehow, the time passed. Recess drew closer. Fuzzy ran laps in his cage, counting down the minutes.

Finally, the bell rang. Kids rushed out the door to play. Digging his decoy out of the pine shavings he'd piled over it, Fuzzy dragged the dummy into his igloo. He got ready to break out of his cage. And then he noticed—

Miss Wills hadn't left the room.

She sat at the desk, puttering away, as if she had all the time in the world. Fuzzy glanced at the clock. Three minutes had passed. He looked at the ceiling tile his friends would come through.

"Come on, come on!" he squeaked.

The teacher glanced up, and he jumped to block her view of the dummy.

"I know, little guy," said Miss Wills with an understanding nod. "You're going to miss us while we're gone."

"Not exactly," said Fuzzy.

He checked the ceiling tile. Somehow, he had to warn his friends. If they came tumbling out while the teacher was still here, their whole trip would go up in flames!

But if he left the cage to warn them, Miss Wills would catch him and tighten up security. Fuzzy was stuck. Not for the first time, he wished he could operate a phone. Then, if Fuzzy could only talk human talk like Sassafras, he could call Miss Wills and lure her away from the room.

Of course, he didn't talk human talk. And even if he did, he'd have to get his paws on a phone first.

So much for that bright idea.

Another minute ticked by. Miss Wills began packing up her belongings, moving slower than Marta in wintertime.

There! The ceiling tile moved, sliding out of place.

The other pets were arriving.

Fuzzy had to *do* something. But what?

CHAPTER 13

Marta Flips Out

Fresh out of options, Fuzzy rose to his hind legs, grabbed his chest, and burst out with a hacking cough. *Eh-hock! Uh-huck! Eh-haw!*

"Fuzzy?" said Miss Wills, half rising from her chair.

Eh-hick! Ah-hack! Uh-huck!

He coughed as loudly as he could, hoping to alert the other pets and distract the teacher at the same time. Sassafras's green head poked through the gap in the ceiling. Fuzzy kept hacking and waving his arms to attract her attention.

"Is something wrong?" Miss Wills was approaching his cage.

Spotting the teacher, Sassafras's eyes widened. She ducked back into the crawl space.

Limp with relief, Fuzzy slumped onto the pine shavings. The teacher watched with a wrinkled brow. "Oh no!" she said. "You've caught a cold or something. I'll take you to the vet's right away."

Whoops, my acting's too good! thought Fuzzy. He had to relieve her worries, and quickly, or he'd miss out on the whole trip.

Giving one last *gack*, as if clearing something from his throat, Fuzzy shook himself. He strolled over to his water dish, drank, and then peered up at the teacher with an innocent, adorable look that would've given Cinnabun a run for her money.

Slipping a finger between the bars, Miss Wills stroked his fur. "Are you okay, little guy?" she asked. "Maybe some hay went down the wrong way?"

Fuzzy purred, cranking up the adorability.

"Huh. You seem all right now," said the teacher, still not entirely convinced. An electronic warble sounded, and Miss Wills fished a phone from her pocket. "Hello? Yes? Oh, thank you. I'll be right there."

With a last glance at Fuzzy, she hung up and headed for the door. It closed behind her with a *snick*.

"Okay," Fuzzy called. "It's safe now."

In a flutter of orange and green, Sassafras glided down from the ceiling and landed on the cage. "I thought she'd never leave," she squawked.

"Hurry!" cried Fuzzy. "There's only twelve minutes left."

They sprang into action. While Sassafras flew over to the cubbyholes and unzipped some book bags for them to hide in, Fuzzy slipped out of his cage and guided the other animals down.

"That's the way," he told Igor and Mistletoe. "Right down the bookshelf and along the cactus."

"Are you totally whackadoodle?" said Igor. "Cactuses hurt."

"Not plastic ones," said Fuzzy.

He watched as the two pets descended the bookcase, followed a minute later by Cinnabun. Somehow she made the whole awkward process of scrambling down the furniture look as graceful as an all-flamingo ballet.

"Wow, she's smooth," said Mistletoe, pausing atop the cubbyholes to admire the bunny.

Fuzzy snorted. He himself had fallen the first five times he'd taken that escape route. "She's all right," he said, checking the clock. "But there's just seven minutes left before the kids come back. Where's Marta and Luther?"

The other pets joined him by the cubbyholes, staring up anxiously. For what seemed like forever, nothing happened. When at last the tortoise poked her head through the gap in the ceiling, everyone cheered.

"There she is!" squawked Sassafras. "The tortoise with the mostest!"

"She's making a dramatic entrance," cooed Cinnabun, "just like a movie star."

"Like a slowpoke," muttered Igor. Fuzzy elbowed him.

"Hurry!" called Mistletoe helpfully.

As they watched, Luther the boa extended himself down from the ceiling onto the bookshelf, and Marta, moving ever so gingerly, descended him like a staircase. "Ow!" said the snake. "Watch the claws!"

"Begging your pardon," said Marta. When she reached the top of the metal bookcase, she peeked over the edge and blanched. "Oh my." She gulped. "That's a long way down."

"Easy peasy," chirped Sassafras. "We all made it just fine."

The tortoise shot her a sour look. "I'm sure you did. On wings. But turtles aren't exactly climbers."

"Well, with Brother Luther to lend a hand—" Cinnabun began.

"Uh, totally hands-free here," said the snake, forming a stair to the next shelf down. "Always have been."

The bunny dimpled prettily. "I do apologize. Figure of speech. With Luther's help, we'll have you down here in two shakes of a lamb's tail," she told Marta.

That might have been a slight exaggeration. Timid and deliberate, the tortoise took her sweet time descending to each shelf, moving at the pace of paint drying.

Fuzzy kept an eye on the clock as the seconds ticked past.

Five minutes.

Four minutes.

"Hurry, hurry!" squeaked a jittery Mistletoe. "There's only three minutes left!"

Through gritted teeth, Fuzzy said, "Don't worry, Marta. Nice and easy now."

Cinnabun addressed the other pets. "Perhaps we should take our positions?" she said. "Just in case?"

Mistletoe scuttled into a book bag so fast, she was just a mouse-shaped blur. Cinnabun and Igor followed suit, and Sassafras zipped up the sacks behind them before seeking her own hiding place.

"Come on, Fuzzy," called the mouse.

"Just a second," he said. "Luther?"

"Yeah, baby?" said the boa.

"Anything you can do to speed it up?"

A sly grin spread across the snake's face. "Oh yeah." He glanced at Marta. "Do you trust me?"

"Why, uh, yes," she said.

"Then hang on."

Wrapping his middle coils around the tortoise, Luther began swinging down the bookcase like a monkey in the treetops. He hooked first his neck, then his tail around the pole supporting the shelves, dropping lower and lower.

"Ugh, I'm . . . dizzy," said Marta. Her eyes bugged out. "Getting . . . seasick."

Fuzzy's heart hammered. He gnawed his knuckles and kept glancing from the clock to his friends. "Almost there," he called.

At last, Luther reached the floor. Unwrapping his coils, he released Marta, who wobbled sideways like a crab.

"Still . . . dizzy," she said.

"This way," said Fuzzy. "Hurry!"

The tortoise staggered, stumbled, and somehow flipped onto her back, legs waving.

And right at that moment, the class bell rang.

BRRRRINNNG!

Holy haystacks! Fuzzy leaped straight up into the air with an alarmed *wheek!*

"Go, go, go!" squawked Sassafras, who'd poked her head out of a book bag.

Fuzzy whipped around to watch the door. The kids would be coming in any moment now. If Marta didn't hurry, they'd catch her in the act.

"We're out of time!" he cried, dashing toward the tortoise. At the last second, he leaped into the air with a cry of "Sorry, Marta!" and landed his full weight on the edge of her upturned shell.

Marta flipped upward, balanced for a second on the very rim . . .

And flopped down onto her back again.

Voices echoed in the hallway, drawing nearer.

"Luther, help!" cried Fuzzy.

Together they raised up and plunged down against Marta's shell again. This time, she flipped all the way over—right on top of them.

"Oof!" cried Fuzzy, smashed flat. He'd never tried lifting a tortoise before, and now he knew why. "Can you . . . move a little?" he gasped.

"No time," said Luther. "We'll have to carry her."

With a supreme effort, Fuzzy struggled up onto his feet. Together, he and the boa slither-staggered toward the cubbyholes as fast as they could.

Wiggling her legs in the air, Marta cried, "Hey, whoa! Tortoises don't run."

"They do now," said Luther.

Miss Wills's voice rang right outside the door, ordering her students into a line.

It was now or never.

Luckily, Sassafras had opened a book bag on the lowest shelf. Fuzzy and the snake stuffed Marta inside, and Fuzzy zipped it closed—just as a key clattered in the lock.

"Go, Luther!" Fuzzy whispered.

In a salmon-colored blur, the snake slithered into a nearby book bag.

The door swung open, unleashing a tide of noise. Fuzzy dove for Mistletoe's hideout. As Miss Wills stepped into the room surrounded by excited students, he closed up the bag behind him as best he could.

"Burrow deep!" he whispered. He and Mistletoe worked their way to the bottom of the compartment and froze.

"Don't forget your book bags," came Miss Wills's muffled instructions. "Hurry now, the bus is waiting."

Someone slid Fuzzy's book bag out and swung it onto a shoulder with a *whump*. Mistletoe, Fuzzy, and a bunch of lunch items tried to occupy the same space at the same time.

Shoving a water bottle away, Fuzzy whispered, "You okay?"

"Indeedy do!" Mistletoe replied.

Fuzzy braced himself against the canvas, holding on tight.

And they were off on their adventure.

CHAPTER 14

Bagging It

Who knew that a field trip involved so much swaying and thumping? Fuzzy and Mistletoe clung together as the book bag thudded against the student's back, mashing them into a sack lunch, a bag of chips, and a bottled water. With every step, they whipped back and forth like an angry cat's tail.

It was hot; it was claustrophobic; it was dizzying.

Several times, Mistletoe squeaked in alarm.

"Shh!" Fuzzy tried shushing her. Fortunately, the kids were chattering so loudly they wouldn't have heard anything short of cannon fire.

After a long, nerve-wracking walk, Fuzzy smelled oily exhaust fumes. He felt the *bip-bip-bip* as the student carrying them climbed a few steps and then a deep rumble that seemed to rise all the way from the floor.

"What's that?" whimpered Mistletoe. "A grizzly bear?"

"I doubt it," said Fuzzy. "There'd be more screaming."

Instead, the kids gabbed happily, laughing and teasing. With another *whump*, Fuzzy's bag landed on something padded—a seat, maybe?

"I think it's the bus," he murmured.

"Really?" Huddling closer, the mouse said, "Then I'm not sure I like buses."

After more ear-splitting jabber and a reminder from Miss Wills about how to behave on a field trip, Fuzzy heard a hiss of air and a thump. With a grinding noise and another seat-shaking rumble, the bus drove off.

"We did it!" Fuzzy whispered. "We're on our way!" Excitement bubbled up in him like one of Miss Wills's more successful science experiments.

In the dimness of the book bag, Mistletoe's face reflected terror and exhilaration. "I hope everyone is okay."

Fuzzy listened closely. It was hard to make out any-thing over the roar of the bus engine and the babble of kids' voices. But since he didn't hear any screams of "What's this in my bag?" he figured they were safe so far.

Tuning into the nearest conversation, Fuzzy guessed that they were sitting with Natalia and Zoey-with-the-braces. Zoey was saying how she wanted to camp out in the dinosaur exhibit and sleep there, she loved them so much. Natalia was more interested in geology, which sounded like the study of rocks.

As far as Fuzzy knew, rocks were for climbing on. Period.

Humans were funny.

The bag swayed as the bus rounded a couple of curves. Fuzzy was burning to see where they were headed.

"What are you doing?" asked Mistletoe.

"Taking a peek," said Fuzzy. "Don't worry."

Ever so cautiously, he climbed toward the slightly open mouth of the book bag and peered out. He blinked, eyes adjusting to the bright sunlight.

Fuzzy caught sight of a bus window and beyond it, glimpses of blue sky and green trees. Brand-new territory!

His heart swelled, and he had to suppress a *wheek*. Now *this* was a proper adventure.

Getting comfortable, Fuzzy drank in the view. This would be the first of many outings, he thought. The pets could go to a theme park, a zoo—maybe even New York City itself.

His daydream was rudely interrupted when the bag gave a sudden lurch and a hand groped at the opening. *Wiggling whiskers!* In a flash, Fuzzy burrowed back down to the bottom.

"—can have a snack before we get there," came Natalia's voice. "I've got corn chips in my lunch."

In dismay, Fuzzy and Mistletoe watched the girl's hand plunge through the opening. It began groping its way down to them like a blinded monster in a horror movie.

"What do we do?" Mistletoe whimpered.

"Just keep out of the way," whispered Fuzzy, jamming himself into a corner.

The hand groped right and left. "Now where are those chips?" said Natalia. Her fingers brushed past the sack lunch, fumbling farther down toward

Mistletoe and Fuzzy. He knew exactly how she'd react when she felt a warm, furry body.

One scream, and the jig would be up.

Spotting the corn chips wedged underneath the lunch bag, Fuzzy dove across the cramped space. He yanked on the packet—once, twice, three times—and it came free. Lunging back the other way, he lifted the chips above his head.

Just then, the bus hit a dip in the road and the seat jounced, launching Fuzzy upward and the snack into Natalia's palm.

"Ah, here we go," she said. Her hand withdrew, holding the corn chips.

Rubber legged, Fuzzy collapsed beside Mistletoe.

"Zip-a-dee-doo!" the mouse whispered. "That was close."

Fuzzy panted, "Too . . . close." He sprawled at the bottom of the bag, his fur standing on end and his heart pit-a-patting like a tap-dancing tarantula.

Whew. This adventure stuff sure took a lot out of a guy.

Given his narrow squeaker, Fuzzy decided to keep a low profile until they were inside the museum. Escaping was a bit trickier than the movies let on, and if he wanted to stick around to enjoy the whole trip, he couldn't take any extra chances.

"Hey," whispered Mistletoe after a while. "What's the museum like?"

"It's got bones of dinosaurs and animals from a long time ago," said Fuzzy.

"And what else?"

"Um, well, it's a natural history museum, so there's lots of historical stuff and also . . . um, natural stuff," said Fuzzy.

"Like rocks and trees?" said the mouse.

"Sure. Probably. Human stuff too."

Mistletoe's head gave a slow, disbelieving shake. "Wow. And anyone can visit?"

With a shrug, Fuzzy said, "Kids and teachers. But we better be sneaky. I hear they don't like animals."

The mouse frowned. "But it's full of animals. Dinosaurs, old tigers . . ."

"I guess they only like dead animals."

This was a sobering thought, which shut both of them up. After a few more minutes of twisty roads, Fuzzy heard the bus squeal and felt it slow down.

"Hey, look!" piped Zoey-with-the-braces. "It's the museum. We're almost there!"

"Cool!" said Natalia.

Fuzzy yearned to poke his head out and see what they were looking at. He wanted to join the excitement, but somehow he managed to stay put.

"Did you hear that?" Mistletoe squeaked. "They can see the museum. I wanna see!" She scrambled up the folds of the book bag toward the opening.

"Wait!" Grabbing her tail with both fists, Fuzzy yanked with all his strength. Down tumbled the mouse.

"What'd you do that for?" she huffed, brushing herself off.

"We've got to keep out of sight, remember?" said Fuzzy. "If they see us, that's it. Game over."

Mistletoe sulked, but she stayed put.

In another couple minutes, the bus stopped, releasing a huge sigh. "Listen up, everyone!" Miss Wills's voice cut through the hubbub. "Bring your bag, stick with your buddy, and follow me. Here we go, kiddos—it's museum time!"

With absolutely no warning, the book bag slid across the seat and lurched into the air. Fuzzy and Mistletoe clutched each other as the contents flew about. Up onto Natalia's shoulder they went with a *whoomp*. Fuzzy hoped the rest of the pets were having an easier ride than he and Mistletoe. Much more of this, and he'd need some of the humans' car-sickness pills.

Down the steps Natalia trotted—*bip-bip-bip*—bouncing them all the way. From the sound of it, fifth graders surrounded them, everyone talking at once. The yummy odor of fresh-cut grass reached Fuzzy's nostrils, and his belly rumbled. They must be just outside the museum.

Bump-bump-bump they went, up a longer flight of stairs. Suddenly, the air grew much cooler and the kids' voices echoed. Was a museum some kind of enormous cave? Fuzzy couldn't wait to see.

"This way!" called Miss Wills from somewhere nearby.

"I'm sorry, ma'am," a man's deep voice boomed. "Purses are okay, but your kids will have to leave their bags in the cloakroom."

"Aww," many students chorused.

Fuzzy froze. The cloakroom? What was that? And

how would he and the others get from there into the rest of the museum?

Too late for second thoughts. A short time later, Fuzzy's book bag swung through the air into a pair of hands that smelled like onions. Through the opening, he glimpsed someone tying a green tag to the bag's strap.

"Don't forget your claim ticket, honey," a woman's voice drawled.

The bag swayed to and fro in this museum person's grip and soon landed on a low shelf with a thud that Fuzzy felt in his back molars.

"Where are we?" whispered Mistletoe.

"Shh!" hissed Fuzzy. "I'll take a look."

Another book bag thumped into place beside theirs. Then another. Slowly, cautiously, Fuzzy crept to the opening and peeked out.

A cramped room met his gaze. Jackets dangled above them, hanging from hooks on the walls, and bags like his lay on low shelves all around the space. Nobody seemed to be about, so Fuzzy poked his head out farther.

Through a narrow door, he could just see a section

of counter and the back of a woman dressed in blue. Suddenly, she whipped around with bags in both hands. Fuzzy ducked.

"What is it?" asked the mouse.

"I think all the fifth graders are leaving their bags in this room."

She wriggled her way up beside him. With noses just peeking out, they watched as two women piled sack after sack into the cloakroom. At long last, the humans dropped a final load and sauntered back to stand at their counter, gossiping.

Wriggling out of the book bag, Fuzzy and Mistletoe surveyed the room. At least a hundred bags and sacks of various sizes surrounded them.

"Where is everyone?" asked the mouse.

Fuzzy gulped. How in the world were they supposed to find the rest of the pets among all these book bags?

CHAPTER 15

The Ghost with the Most

"Hello?" Fuzzy whispered, climbing over the nearby bags. "Igor? Marta? Anybody?"

A muffled noise came from a book bag on the shelf below him.

"Who's there?" he asked, clambering down.

"Only the coolest boa north of the Amazon," said Luther. He poked the tip of his nose through a quarter-sized gap in the zipper. "Help a brother out?"

Fuzzy unzipped the bag, and the snake slithered into the room, twisting his neck this way and that to work out the kinks.

"Oh baby, my spine feels like five miles of bad road," said Luther. "Who was carrying me, a bronco buster?"

"Help me find the others," said Fuzzy.

Between the three of them, they located the rest of the pets and managed to release them. Sassafras looked rumpled, Igor was dizzy, and Marta was even greener than usual. But Cinnabun stepped out as fresh and perfect as if she were walking onto the set of her own TV show.

"What a delightful nap," she said. "I swear, whoever carried me was the gentlest, most delicate soul."

Fuzzy shook his head, disgusted. *Of course* she got the best ride.

The pets gathered together out of sight of the front counter.

"So?" asked Sassafras. "Where are the dinosaurs?"

Fuzzy forced a smile. "Very close," he said. "Ah, just one small problem."

"You bit somebody," said Igor.

"No," said Fuzzy. "Why on earth would you think that?"

The iguana shrugged. "'Problem' usually means somebody bit somebody, or somebody pooped where they weren't supposed to."

"Neither one, thank you," said Fuzzy. "But we do have to sneak past two humans to reach the exhibits."

The pets peeked around the corner at the women in blue, then returned to their nook to confer. "There seems to be no other way out but past those two ladies," said Cinnabun. "Any thoughts?"

"Let's all make a break for it at once," said Sassafras. "If we scatter, they can't catch us." Marta sent her a reproachful look. "Oh, sorry, Marta."

The tortoise harrumphed.

Luther lazily uncoiled himself. "How about I just turn up underfoot? They scream and run, and all of you slip out, smooth as a fresh-laid egg. That'd work."

"Except for one thing," said Igor. "Who knows why, but some people actually *like* snakes. What if these humans do too?"

Stumped for the moment, the pets stared blankly at one another.

Fuzzy considered their strengths—Sassafras's ability to speak human, Cinnabun's cuteness, Mistletoe's nimbleness. He looked around at what they had to work with, mostly book bags and jackets.

Hmm . . .

"What we need," he said, "is a distraction. And I think I know what kind." Fuzzy explained what he had in mind.

Cinnabun wrinkled her nose. "Does anyone have a better idea? Anyone? No?" She sighed. "Then I suppose we should try it. But I must say, I feel like we're barking up the wrong tree."

"Guinea pigs don't bark," said Fuzzy. "But thanks for the vote of confidence."

With Sassafras's help, they pulled an orange windbreaker down from its hook. Everyone crawled underneath it. The jacket smelled like armpits.

"This is either the dumbest idea in the whole world or sheer genius," said Igor. "And I'm betting on the former."

Working together, the pets spread out the windbreaker so it looked like it was flying, very low, across the floor. And then they crept out the doorway, carrying it over their backs.

Immediately, Sassafras moaned in human talk, like a spirit with a stomachache. "Oooh! *Oooh!* Whooo's got my bodyyy?"

From his post at the neck of the windbreaker, Fuzzy peered upward. The two women jumped back with a shriek. "Aah!" cried the bigger one.

"Sweet Moses!" squealed the other.

Luther made the sleeve ripple at them like a ghostly arm was animating it.

"Yoooouu!" wailed the parakeet. "Did yoooouu take it?"

With a piercing scream, the women fled. "Help! Ghosts! Security!"

Peeping out past the counter, Fuzzy saw them dash across the wide entryway toward a closed door. "Let's move out!" he cried.

As quickly as possible, given Marta's slow pace, the pets headed around the corner into the museum proper, with the jacket still held above them. When they'd passed beyond the entryway, they dropped it.

"Gee," said Igor. "Humans are much more gullible than I thought."

"Quick, over here!" squeaked Mistletoe, scampering for the shelter of a pillar. The other pets followed as fast as they were able. Fuzzy and Luther helped Marta along.

From this makeshift cover, Fuzzy took in the museum. His jaw dropped. It was *enormous*! Pillars soared to a ceiling so high it looked like it should have its own clouds. Broad stairs on one side rose up and up to higher floors. Packs of students and the occasional family bustled here and there, heading for the various halls that branched off the central room.

"Wow," breathed Fuzzy.

"Wowie-wow-wow," said Mistletoe.

"Eh," said Igor. "Compared to the Mayan temples my folks come from, this is nothing."

Everybody shot him a look.

"Okay, okay," he said. "It's not bad."

Then Fuzzy spotted something that really made his spine tingle. A little farther down this side of the vast space, an impossibly long-necked creature made all of bone towered nearly to the ceiling. Behind it, above a wide doorway, a sign proclaimed: HALL OF DINOSAURS.

"Dinosaurs!" chirped Sassafras. Her voice went hushed and respectful. "Hello, apatosaurus."

"How do we get over there?" Marta asked, watching a cluster of students vanish into the exhibit room.

A wide stretch of polished floor yawned between their pillar and the hall. People came and went in waves and dribbles, with no way to predict the traffic flow. How could this many animals sneak inside without being seen?

"I know," said Mistletoe, rubbing her paws together. "See how the lights cast shadows near the wall? Just follow me, and I'll get you there."

"What makes you such an expert?" said Igor.

"Ever heard the phrase 'quiet as a mouse'?"

"Yeah?"

Mistletoe indicated herself with both front paws. "*Voilà*, a mouse."

"She's got a point there," said Luther.

The iguana rolled his eyes.

"Move when I move, and stop when I stop," said Mistletoe. "Now, let's go."

Fuzzy was surprised at his little friend's sudden show of leadership. But he followed her along with the others. Three times they froze as people wandered nearby. Each time, the humans shuffled blindly past, their eyes on the marvelous exhibits or signs posted up high.

What a sight we must make, Fuzzy thought. *Three reptiles, a bird, and three mammals, creeping along like the world's strangest spy team.* Just before they reached the dinosaur hall, a commotion behind them made the pets stop and turn. Fuzzy could just make out the humans' words.

"Here it is," said a gray-uniformed security guard, stooping to pick up the abandoned windbreaker. She lifted the jacket and shook it at the blue-suited women. "See? No ghosts."

The cloakroom workers stared suspiciously. "I tell you, Becca," the bigger one said, "it was moving. And we heard a creepy voice, plain as day. Right, Stacie?"

"That's right," said the other one. "*Real* creepy."

The pets stayed frozen in place until the three museum employees eventually turned and retreated the way they'd come, still discussing the "ghost." Fuzzy blew out a sigh. They hadn't been spotted.

Finally, the way was clear. Mistletoe led them into the massive Hall of Dinosaurs, and everyone's jaw dropped with a collective "Whoa!"

In his wildest imagination, Fuzzy had never pictured anything so grand. Staggeringly huge figures dominated the long room. Some dinosaurs were all bone; some wore a painted skin; but all were *amazing*. Dramatic spotlights illuminated the beasts, casting convenient pools of shadow for the pets to hide in.

"Meet my family," said Igor.

"Don't you mean *my* family?" said Sassafras. "Birds are the ones who came from dinos, after all."

"That's ridiculous. I *look* like a dinosaur."

The parakeet made a mock-pitying face. "Aw, haven't your first graders learned yet how animals evolve? Maybe if you were in a fourth-grade class like me . . ."

Igor stuck out his tongue at her and returned his attention to the great beasts.

They saw triceratops and pterodactyl, stegosaurus and diplodocus. But the most impressive one of all, looming above the rest, was Tyrannosaurus rex.

When she first caught sight of the fearsome creature, Mistletoe squeaked and scooted behind Fuzzy.

"Really?" he said.

She peeked out at it. "Sorry," she said. "Instinct."

He went back to gaping at the colossus. "Wiggling whiskers, those teeth are longer than I am!"

After the dinosaur hall, they wandered through the

Hall of Meteorites, the nature photography gallery, and the ocean life exhibit. They marveled at each new wonder. Twice, the group crossed paths with Leo Gumpus students, but both times the pets remained undetected.

Fuzzy and the rest—even Igor—gaped at the sights.

"Well, slather me with butter and call me a biscuit," Cinnabun murmured. "Who knew the world was such an amazing place?"

Speechless, Fuzzy could only nod.

When the pets entered the Hall of Human Origins, Sassafras burst out with an earsplitting cackle that could've been heard in Bolivia. "Hilarious!" she squawked. "Look, they're so furry!"

"Shh!" said Fuzzy.

"What's wrong with furry?" asked Mistletoe.

"SHH!"

But the humans had heard Sassafras's outcry. Searching for the source of the noise, many visitors turned toward them. Fuzzy clamped a paw over Sassafras's beak. All the pets crouched low. (Except for Luther, who was already as low as he could go.)

Across the room, a couple complained loudly, pointing in their direction. The same blonde, gray-uniformed guard they'd seen earlier made a calming gesture and strode toward the pets.

"Hide!" whispered Mistletoe.

Fuzzy scanned the room. No rocks, no crevices, no convenient nooks.

They were caught in the open like a rat under a hungry hawk.

CHAPTER 16

Neanderthal Noah's Ark

"Follow my lead!" cried Fuzzy. Whirling, he darted beneath the guardrail, directly into the nearest diorama, "Neanderthal Life." Stiff figures of cavemen posed against a realistic-looking forest background.

As the other pets piled in and the guard drew nearer, Fuzzy whispered, "Strike a pose, and freeze!"

"What?" said Marta.

"Freeze!"

Demonstrating, he set his front feet on a fake log and went rigid. From the corner of an eye, he could see the museum employee approach, swiveling her head to spot anything out of place. The two visitors trailed her.

"It was a bizarre jungle sound," said the first visitor, a bearded man as skinny as a stick of chalk. "So loud it startled us. They've never played that kind of soundtrack in here before."

"We still don't," said the blonde guard, who Fuzzy remembered was called Becca. She stopped right in front of him, taking in the exhibits and the human visitors in a 360-degree scan.

He tried to control his trembling.

Just a few steps beyond him, Cinnabun and Luther had frozen, mid-run. It looked like the bunny was chasing the boa.

Beardy Guy leaned forward, squinting. "I don't recall seeing these animals in here before. And why is a rabbit pursuing a snake? That's not realistic."

Becca gave the animals a strange look, then shrugged. "Beats me," she said. "That's the Exhibit Department's job."

"Well, they're doing their job wrong," said the man.

"Now, Milton," his partner said.

Milton, a.k.a. Beardy Guy, indicated Fuzzy with contempt. "Guinea pigs!" he huffed. "They're not even found in the Old World. What's he supposed to be, on vacation?"

"Sir," the guard began.

"And parakeets? Really?" Milton spluttered. "I-I-Is this some sort of demented Neanderthal Noah's Ark?"

"Okay, sir." Becca's smile was showing signs of strain. "I'll mention that to Exhibits. I'm sure there's a reason for it."

Beardy Milton huffed. "Certainly there is. They've gone stark-raving bonkers!"

With an embarrassed grimace, the man with him put an arm around Milton's shoulders and steered him away. "He gets cranky when he needs a snack," he said. "Blood sugar. Come along, Milton."

The guard watched them leave, and Fuzzy sagged in relief. At the slight movement, Becca's head whipped back around. He stiffened again.

Had she seen him stir? Fuzzy's heart hammered like a woodpecker in a coffee plantation, and his eyes bulged in fear.

Everything in him wanted to bolt for safety. But somehow, Fuzzy held stock-still for several long moments as the security guard stared from him to the other pets with a frown.

Just when Fuzzy thought his heart would explode, the woman shook her head and relaxed. "Ghosts and exhibit pranks?" Becca muttered. "What is *with* everyone today?"

This time, Fuzzy kept his pose as the guard strolled away and out of the room. A band of four kids passed by, staring with no comment.

"Can we move now?" came Mistletoe's lock-jawed voice from somewhere close behind. "I got a cramp."

Fuzzy's gaze scanned the room. Clear—for the moment. "Let's move," he said. "Quick, now."

As one, the pets slipped out of the brightly lit exhibit and back into the shadows. Cinnabun fanned herself. "Well, fry my hide!" she said. "That was just too close for little old me. I'm simply not used to that sort of excitement."

With a wing, Sassafras helped fan her. Luther murmured, "There, there, Missy Miss," in a soothing voice.

The bunny's eyelids fluttered prettily. "I—I'm not sure how much more of this I can handle." She really seemed to be milking it.

Fuzzy snorted. "This is adventure: excitement, thrills, close calls. Maybe you shouldn't have come."

"No, no," said Cinnabun, allowing Igor and Luther to support her elbows. "I'm just feeling a tad faint. I need . . . refreshment."

"Food!" Mistletoe piped up. "I'm on it." She scurried off while the rest of the pets moved the rabbit into a secluded corner, where their club president could recuperate out of sight.

Fuzzy tapped his foot. Would they miss out on the rest of the museum's wonders, all because of Cinnabun? Once more, he pictured ditching her in some back room of the museum, and felt himself smile.

That wasn't so wrong, was it? After all, with her cuteness factor, some human would find her and adopt her in a hot second.

Soon, the mouse scampered back and rejoined the group. "There's a snack shack in the courtyard just around the corner. I already borrowed an apple—it's easy!"

She led them out of the exhibit hall and into the museum's spacious courtyard. Here, several food carts sold all sorts of eats, and visitors sat at scattered tables.

Not far off, Fuzzy spotted Miss Wills and her class, happily munching away on their meals.

"Guess it wouldn't hurt to have some lunch," he mumbled.

Marta looked up at all the humans stomping past them. She dodged a careless foot. "But first, we need a safe place to eat it."

Sassafras's sharp eyes spotted a garden in the corner, full of lush ferns and broad-leafed bushes. "And the plucky parakeet comes through again! Follow me, ladies and germs."

In less time than it normally took Marta to blow her nose, the pets were settled beneath leafy plants, safe from prying eyes. Mistletoe came staggering back, carrying an apple that dwarfed her, and dropped it at Cinnabun's feet.

"Oh, you're too kind," cooed the bunny. "I don't suppose they have any crispy lettuce?"

The mouse and parakeet returned to the snack shacks to scavenge some more tidbits. Soon, there was enough for everyone to eat—fruits, veggies, and even some of those baked treats that humans were so clever about making.

As he nibbled a piece of apple, something occurred to Fuzzy. "We don't know when they're leaving," he said aloud.

"Say what?" asked Luther.

"The fifth graders," said Fuzzy. "The ones we're riding home with? We don't know what time they leave."

Cinnabun's eyes widened. "Oh my stars! Well, someone should certainly find that out." She stared pointedly at Fuzzy.

"Yes, someone should," he said. "That's my point."

The bunny gazed at him some more, joined by Marta, Luther, and Igor.

"Oh, all right," Fuzzy grumbled. "I'll go listen in, see what I can learn."

"Bless your heart," said Cinnabun. "Such a brave volunteer. Don't you agree, Brother Luther?"

The boa grinned. "I'd say amen."

Fuzzy sighed. He hadn't realized that leading an adventure meant you had to do most of the work. Off through the bushes he trudged.

Fortunately, Miss Wills's table was near enough to the garden that he could eavesdrop without being seen.

Fuzzy took a post under a shaggy bush and settled in to listen.

"—and be sure to clean up after yourselves," the teacher was telling the students at her table. "Remember, when we're on a field trip, we represent Leo Gumpus Elementary."

"Yes, Miss Wills," the fifth graders mumbled.

She made a face. "I know you know this already. I just want us to make a good impression."

Fuzzy considered what kind of impression the pets would make, showing up in the middle of the museum in all their glory. He decided he'd rather not find out.

The students who'd finished eating began collecting their trash. Heavy-Handed Jake, at the nearest table, popped the top off his soda cup and tossed the remains of his drink into the bushes—right onto Fuzzy.

Sploosh! Ice and sticky-sweet soda rained down. Fuzzy shuddered and shook himself all over. He was drenched.

"There," said Jake. "Now I can recycle the cup."

As the students rose to go, Miss Wills said, "Don't forget, we leave here at two fifteen. That means everyone meets by the cloakroom at two o'clock. Got it?"

"Rodger-dodger, over and out," said Malik, who loved spy movies. He pretended to fiddle with something on his wrist. "Watches synchronized."

Maya made a face. "You don't have a watch."

"I know," said Malik. "But I always wanted to say that."

The mention of spies reminded Fuzzy. It was time to sneak away before he was spotted, and share his information with the other pets. He crept off through the ferns.

"What happened to you?" Igor cackled when he arrived. "Museum Jacuzzi?"

"Recycling accident," said Fuzzy. He told them about the departure plans. "So we need to be back inside those book bags before two o'clock."

"Piece of cake," said Sassafras.

"Where?" asked Mistletoe eagerly.

The parakeet clucked. "Figure of speech. It's a snap—there's plenty of time to see more before we go."

After a heated discussion about which exhibits to visit, they decided to split into two groups. Igor, Luther, Marta, and Sassafras were keen on checking out Birds and Reptiles, while the rest wanted to see the Hall of Mammals.

"But before we go," said Cinnabun, "there's just one more thing I need, to restore my spirits."

Fuzzy frowned. "What's that?"

A dazzling smile spread across the bunny's face. "Let's sing a few verses of 'Happy Happy Boogaloo' and do a quick who's-the-cutest-in-the-museum contest."

Fuzzy rolled his eyes so hard he thought they'd get stuck. "But we don't have time—"

"Fiddlesticks," said Cinnabun. "No one can see us here in the garden, and we've got oodles of time." She pouted prettily and made with the melty eyes. "It would mean ever so much to me."

The other pets gave in immediately.

All through that annoying song and the cuteness contest (which Cinnabun won—no surprise), Fuzzy felt a headache brewing. He thought of all the cool sights they were missing. He tapped his foot and drummed his fingers, but the bunny wouldn't be hurried.

After what seemed like an ice age later, the group finally divided. Cinnabun and Mistletoe led the way to the Hall of Mammals, chatting merrily about whether Alvin and the Chipmunks or Puss in Boots was cuter.

Trailing behind, Fuzzy shot a dark look at Cinnabun's

back. The opportunity was at hand. The situation was nearly perfect. He had put up with her cuteness and silliness and irritating rabbit-ness long enough.

Well, no more.

Time to begin Operation Bye-Bye Bunny.

CHAPTER 17

Take the Bunny and Run

Their visit to the Hall of Mammals started innocently enough. Fuzzy, Mistletoe, and Cinnabun *ooh*ed and *aah*ed at prehistoric creatures like the mastodon, saber-toothed tiger, and woolly rhinoceros. They mourned extinct animals like the Tasmanian tiger and Eurasian wild horse. They marveled at the world's smallest (bumblebee bat) and largest (blue whale) mammals.

As the trio slipped through the shadows of the long gallery, Fuzzy racked his brain. All he had to do was split up his group. If he could misdirect Cinnabun, she'd arrive too late to stow away for the trip home.

Good-bye, rabbit problem; hello, President Fuzzy.

A teeny-tiny voice inside him whispered that this was maybe a mean thing to do to a fellow pet. But the thought of her obnoxious cuteness drowned it out.

He waited until Mistletoe and Cinnabun were busy admiring different exhibits, and he edged up beside the bunny. "If we get separated for any reason, let's meet up with everyone else at that Neanderthal scene."

"Sounds like a splendid idea," said Cinnabun.

Right after that, Fuzzy gave Mistletoe the same message, but told her to meet at the cloakroom instead. He felt a slight twinge at deceiving the rabbit, but he believed that all the other pets would welcome the end of sing-alongs and cuteness contests.

Yes, he was playing a mean trick. But it was for the good of the club, right?

Now that the groundwork had been laid, Fuzzy watched for the chance to set his plan in motion. He didn't have long to wait. The three pets had made their way to the Australian mammal collection and were gaping at the kangaroos from the safety of shadows.

Suddenly, a little boy came skipping along from the neighboring koala display and nearly ran into them.

He stopped dead, gaping. "A bunny rabbit!" he cried. "Mommy, a real-live bunny!"

The boy dived for Cinnabun, grabbing air as she leaped aside.

"Split up!" yelled Fuzzy. "We'll meet back at the place!"

All three pets lunged in different directions. As Fuzzy sprinted for a side passage, he saw Mistletoe scooting into the kangaroo exhibit, and Cinnabun fleeing the boy and his mother.

"Get it, Mommy!" the brat whined. "Wanna wanna bunny rabbit!"

"Hey, guard!" another visitor cried. "There's a critter loose in here!"

Fuzzy bit his lip. He hated to leave a fellow pet in such a tight spot, but if Cinnabun got caught, she'd probably find a nice new home far away from Leo Gumpus. Besides, all was fair in politics and war.

Hugging the shadows, he fled for the cloakroom.

The museum seemed even busier than it had earlier that morning. Several times, Fuzzy had to wait forever for the coast to clear before dashing across exposed stretches of floor. Even worse, as he entered the main hall, it seemed like Becca, the blonde guard, had spotted him.

Fuzzy froze, hoping against hope that he was wrong.

But then she trotted over, and he slipped around behind a pillar, his heart in his mouth. Ready to bolt, Fuzzy watched both sides of the column. When her shadow showed on one side, he went the other way. The guard began circling, and Fuzzy hustled to keep ahead of her.

Around and around they went, like the monkey chasing the weasel. At last, a visitor called the guard away. Fuzzy waited until his heartbeat returned to something approaching normal, and then he forged onward.

The entryway's big clock read 1:52 when he reached the cloakroom. A few of the fifth graders were milling around in front of the counter, waiting for their friends to arrive. Had they reclaimed their bags yet? Fuzzy checked. It didn't look like it. Still time to stow away.

Only one worker staffed the counter. When she entered the room to fetch a visitor's checked item, Fuzzy slipped in on her heels. The woman lifted a jacket off its hanger and turned.

Yikes! Fuzzy dove beneath the nearest shelf. Without a second glance, the worker strode past him and out the doorway. He slumped, frazzled.

A snake's head poked out of the bag beside him.

Wheek! Fuzzy jumped straight up with a shriek.

"Hey, Fuzzmeister," said Luther, "maybe you ought to lay off the coffee drinks."

Clutching his chest, Fuzzy gasped, "Don't sneak up on me like that."

"I'm a snake," said the boa. "It's what we do."

"Is everyone in their bags?"

Luther nodded. "All us bird and reptile types, anyhow. Your group?"

"Uh, yeah," said Fuzzy, with a guilty twinge. "All good to go."

He waited while the museum worker reclaimed another jacket. Then, Fuzzy darted for the shelter of his own book bag.

Mistletoe was waiting. "At last!" she squeaked. "I was so worried. Did Cinnabun make it back too?"

"Um, sure," said Fuzzy, turning away. His throat felt tight and his stomach queasy. This made no sense—

getting rid of the pesky rabbit was supposed to be a happy-making thing, right?

Just then, a firm hand hoisted their hiding place into the air, and both pets fell silent. They felt the familiar disorienting sway as the worker passed Natalia the bag, and the thump as the girl slung it over a shoulder. Then came the *bump-bump-bump* of trotting down the museum steps, and the shorter *bip-bip-bip* of climbing onto the bus. As before, the vehicle reverberated with the noise of kids laughing, yelling, and rehashing their museum experiences.

"Thank you, Fuzzy," said Mistletoe.

"For what?"

"That was fun-fun-fun!" The mouse's grin glowed in the dimness of the book bag. "I never knew a museum could be so exciting!"

"Yeah," said Fuzzy. "It was pretty cool, all right."

But something distracted him from savoring the sweetness of their accomplishment. He'd reached his dream. He should be ecstatic. But for some reason, Fuzzy just couldn't get Cinnabun out of his head.

"You know," said Mistletoe, "she really admires you."

Fuzzy blinked. "Er, who does?"

"Our president, Cinnabun."

Fuzzy shook his head. He must have heard wrong. "You mean Little Miss Perfect? The one who's obsessed with cuteness?"

"Well, yeah," said Mistletoe. "What other Cinnabun is there? She said she thinks you're the bee's knees."

Trying to get comfortable, Fuzzy nudged the water bottle aside. "Really? Why?"

Mistletoe squinched up her nose, searching her memory. "She said you were . . . bold and courageous, willing to take chances. Cinnabun wishes she was more like you."

When Fuzzy tried to talk, he discovered a lump in his throat the size of a softball. He was speechless. The queen of charm, the bunny who had it all, wished she could be more like *him*?

An image sprang to mind of the last time he'd seen her—fleeing from a bratty kid and his mom. He, Fuzzy, had abandoned her to her fate. Was that the action of someone bold? Was that the way a future Class Pets president behaved? Obnoxious or not, no pet deserved to be left the way he'd left her.

160

Clamping his eyes shut, Fuzzy massaged his forehead.

"Are you okay?" asked Mistletoe.

"I . . . I'm going back in," he said.

The mouse's eyes bulged. "What? We're just about to leave."

Fuzzy gripped her shoulders. "Cinnabun didn't make it out. I left her behind, and now I have to go get her."

"Holy cheesesticks!"

"Tell the other pets," said Fuzzy. "Cause a diversion, delay the bus."

"Me?" said Mistletoe. "I can't—uh, what kind of diversion?"

"You're a smart mouse; you'll think of something. Just don't let them leave until we return."

"But, but . . ."

Fuzzy looked her in the eye. "Can I count on you, Mistletoe?"

Her lips pursed. Slowly, she nodded. "Aye-aye, Captain!"

With a last clap to her shoulder, Fuzzy wriggled his way up to the opening. He peeked outside. Nobody was watching, so he sneaked out of the bag and dropped onto the floor.

"People, may I have your attention, please?" came Miss Wills's voice. "I need to call roll and make sure we've got everyone."

Dodging between feet and backpacks, Fuzzy scurried under the seats, heading for the door.

"Amir?" said the teacher.

"Present," said the boy.

Someone shifted their feet, and Fuzzy narrowly

avoided being punted by a pair of sneakers. He dodged and kept going.

"Ava?" said Miss Wills.

"Here," said Ava.

Fuzzy had nearly reached the front of the bus. He could see Miss Wills's rainbow-colored tennis shoes planted in the aisle. How could he slip around her without being spotted?

"Brandon?" said the teacher.

"A mouse!" Loud Brandon squealed.

"Excuse me?" said Miss Wills.

"A snake!" cried Ava.

The bus exploded in pandemonium. Darting between Miss Wills's feet, Fuzzy leaped down the steps one by one. The last was kind of high, but he flung himself off, landing on the sidewalk with a breathtaking *whump*.

Up a wide flight of stairs loomed the museum, a building big enough to hold a hundred whales with room left over for a Tyrannosaurus tea party. Fuzzy set his jaw and narrowed his eyes. Somewhere inside that museum was a scared, obnoxiously cute bunny named Cinnabun.

And it was up to him to rescue her.

CHAPTER 18

Mission: Improbable

What would those guys in The Great Escape *do?* Fuzzy asked himself. How would they pull off a rescue? They'd probably disguise themselves as museum guards and zoom into the building on souped-up motorcycles.

He looked around. No guinea pig–sized uniforms or miniature motorcycles to be seen—just some random humans milling about. Fuzzy sighed. Why couldn't life be more like the movies?

The steps looked awfully daunting. Each one stood taller than Fuzzy on his hind legs, and he was not the world's greatest climber. He gnawed his lip. There had to be an easier way in.

Just then, a woman in a motorized wheelchair rolled right in front of him, headed for the corner of the building. He squinted at it. A ramp there wound its way gently up to the museum door. Perfect!

Before he could stop and think, Fuzzy sprinted at the back of the wheelchair as hard as he could.

He leaped and landed on a metal platform beneath the chair. It was hot and vibrating, but Fuzzy clung on, swallowed in a cloud of the woman's flowery perfume. When they motored up to the ticket taker, he crept farther underneath to avoid being seen.

"Come on, come on!" He urged the slowpoke driver to hurry. Who knew how long Mistletoe and the others could delay the bus?

When the wheelchair turned toward the dinosaur exhibit, Fuzzy jumped off and hugged the wall.

A redheaded man spotted him. "Hey!" he called.

Fuzzy tore onward, with the visitor in pursuit. It was touch-and-go for a minute there, but he lost the man around the apatosaurus.

Leaving the dinosaurs behind, he scurried straight for the Hall of Human Origins. Hopefully, Cinnabun was waiting by the Neanderthals as he'd told her. Then, they could just dash back outside, board the bus, and head home, safe and sound.

Racing from shadow to shadow, Fuzzy entered the exhibit hall. A family stood gaping at the caveman display. He waited impatiently until they'd gone and then crept up to the exhibit.

"Cinnabun?" he whispered. "Are you there?" Checking around for witnesses, he called a bit louder. No answer.

A quick check inside the diorama revealed the truth. No bunny.

Fuzzy tugged his whiskers in frustration. Where could she have gone? Time was running out.

He decided to trot over to the mammal exhibits, where he'd seen her last. But just as he entered the main hall, a grating, familiar voice caught his attention.

"Wanna, wanna bunny rabbit!"

It was the bratty boy from before, being dragged toward the exit by his frazzled-looking mother. Maybe they knew something. Fuzzy dodged people's feet to draw closer.

"Wanna *rabbit*!" the boy cried again.

"You can't have the bunny, Boo-Boo," said his mother through a clenched-teeth smile. "The nice guard took it away. How about an ice cream instead?"

Fuzzy gave a little hop of alarm. The security guards had captured Cinnabun! How on earth could he bust her out now?

Stunned at the news, he narrowly avoided being trampled by a tour group in a hurry. Fuzzy shuffled over to the wall and slumped against it.

Well, that was that. He'd given the rescue mission his best shot, hadn't he? Nobody could expect more. After all, it wasn't his fault that Cinnabun had gotten herself caught.

He pulled himself together. Time to get back to the bus, or he'd miss his ride home.

As Fuzzy sneaked along the wall, he noticed a door labeled SECURITY OFFICE up ahead. It was closed, of course, and he was a guinea pig. Opening doors was *way* beyond his abilities—anyone knew that. Why, he couldn't even knock loud enough to be heard.

And then, just as he was about to glide past the door, it opened. Fuzzy went rigid. A mustachioed man in a gray uniform stepped directly over him without noticing and headed across the main hall toward the bathrooms. The door began to swing shut.

Fuzzy darted inside.

Immediately, he scurried for the nearest shelter he could find, which turned out to be a couple of tall cardboard boxes sitting by the wall. He peered between them into the office.

It was an olive-green cave of a room, with a low ceiling, a couple of desks, and scuffed, mismatched furniture. The stale air smelled of cupcakes, coffee, and boredom. Above one desk stretched a bank of video monitors showing black-and-white images from cameras all around the museum. Fuzzy edged farther out. The room was empty.

"Cinnabun!" he cried. "Where are you?"

"*Brother Fuzzy?*" came a voice from right beside him. "I'm here!"

He sniffed and realized that one of the boxes smelled rather rabbit-y. "Can you hop out?"

"I tried," said Cinnabun.

"Well, try again."

A scrabbling sound was followed by a clunk and a thump. "No, I reckon not," said the bunny.

"We've only got a few minutes," said Fuzzy. "That guard is coming right back. Can you chew through the box?"

"I'm afraid the corners face the wrong way," said Cinnabun.

Baffled, Fuzzy pulled his ears. "Think, think!" he muttered.

"I *am* thinking," said the bunny.

"I meant me."

His gaze swept the room, searching, searching . . . and lit upon a long clipboard that sat on the nearer desk. "Hey, if I drop a ramp into your box, could you use it as a springboard to escape?"

"I can certainly try," said Cinnabun.

Fuzzy took a running start and leaped up onto a bookshelf that stood beside the desk. As he clambered up and up, all he could think was: *The guard is coming back; the bus is leaving*.

But still he pressed onward.

When he'd climbed high enough, Fuzzy jumped from

the bookshelf to the desktop. Across its surface he scurried, knocking pens and papers aside. He slipped his front paws under the clipboard, heaved, and levered it up to shoulder height.

Fuzzy cut his eyes over at Cinnabun's box. So close, and yet, so far. How would he ever maneuver the clipboard into it?

Her melty eyes gazed up at him. "Bless your heart for saving me. You are a prince among rodents."

Fuzzy felt a hot flush of shame. "I'm not so great."

"No, seriously," she said. "You're so much braver and bolder than I am. You risked yourself for me."

"Brave, huh?" Fuzzy huffed and jerked, managing to heft the clipboard up onto his head like a surfboard. It balanced precariously as he staggered under its weight. "If I'm such a hero, how come I told you the wrong meeting place?"

Cinnabun pulled her head back. "You what?"

He couldn't bear to look at her anymore. Fuzzy tottered toward the desk's edge, with the clipboard wobbling above him. "I told you the Neanderthal exhibit when it was really the cloakroom."

Her eyes reflected hurt, but her tone was light. "A boyish prank," the bunny scoffed uncertainly. "You are such a kidder."

"I'm not. I was jealous. I'm a bad, bad rodent." Fuzzy paused at the very edge of the desk, muscles straining. At last he met her gaze.

"If you're so all-fired bad," she said, "then what are you doing here now?"

Fuzzy opened his mouth to reply. But just at that moment, the office door swung wide and the mustachioed security guard stepped into the room.

CHAPTER 19

Showdown with Mustache

Fuzzy stared at the man. The man stared at Fuzzy. He was tall and rangy as a basketball player, with a huge mustache that hung from his lip like black moss.

"What the diggity duckwad?" said the guard. Recovering his wits, he rushed toward the desk.

Fuzzy leaned back, and with all his might, flung the clipboard at Cinnabun's box. It ricocheted off the man's outstretched arm, which was a good thing, since Fuzzy's throw was too short. The clipboard flipped through the air and struck the edge of the box, tumbling inside.

"Ouch!" cried Cinnabun.

But Fuzzy had no time to worry about the rabbit. He dodged Mossy Mustache's grab and darted behind the multi-line telephone.

"Come back here, you little rat!" the man yelled.

"I'm no rat; I'm a guinea pig!" Fuzzy squeaked.

A big hand groped around one side of the device, so Fuzzy dashed the other way, toward the desktop computer. Mossy Mustache lunged again, banging his knee on the back of the chair.

"Ow! Dag blast it!" the guard snarled.

From the corner of his eye, Fuzzy caught a blur of white fur streaking over the box. At least Cinnabun was free. Maybe she could escape while he distracted the man.

Fuzzy ducked behind the computer monitor, his heart hammering like an army of carpenters. In another grab, the guard bruised his knuckles. He cussed some more, using words Fuzzy had never heard—not even in the movies.

As Fuzzy gathered himself to make another run for it, he happened to notice a red button on the wall nearby. A small plaque underneath it read IN CASE OF EMERGENCY. *If this isn't an emergency,* he thought, *I don't know what is.*

The next time Mossy Mustache's big hand snatched at him, Fuzzy scrambled right over the man's knuckles and launched himself into the air. Stretching to his limit, he flew toward the button and pounded it with both paws.

WHOOP! WHOOP! WHOOP! An earsplitting alarm began to wail.

Fuzzy dropped to the desktop, spent. A pair of hands closed over him.

"Hey!" he squeaked.

"Gotcha!" growled the guard. He lifted Fuzzy into the air—not holding him with soft hands, but squeezing him like humans squeeze a toothpaste tube.

Suffering mange mites! Fuzzy squirmed and kicked. No use. He wasn't going anywhere; the man held him tighter than a python's embrace.

"You rigga-ragga little troublemaker," Mossy Mustache yelled over the siren's blare. "You're in for it now." His sour breath reeked of pickles.

Fuzzy gulped. With a sinking feeling, he remembered that in *The Great Escape*, most of the runaway prisoners met an unhappy ending. He tried to be brave.

He tried to take comfort in knowing he'd finally tasted real freedom. But he could feel his chin quivering as the man pawed the computer keyboard with one hand.

"How do you turn off this shazz-blasted thing?" growled Mossy Mustache.

When suddenly—

"Yeow!" The guard wailed, jackknifing abruptly. His hand twitched open, and Fuzzy plummeted to the floor, bouncing once off the chair.

Dazed, he shook himself and climbed to his feet.

Cinnabun was wiping her mouth with a paw. As they darted under the desk together, the guard gripped his ankle and hopped about, cussing a blue streak.

Pointing at the man, Fuzzy mimed a bite and raised his eyebrows. When the bunny nodded, he grinned, flashing her the okay sign.

"Pretty darned brave!" he cried over the noise.

"What?" yelled Cinnabun.

The office door banged open. Two gray-uniformed legs strode toward the desk. "What's the emergency?" a woman's voice bellowed.

"Cheese-banged rat got loose!" yelled the man.

"What?"

Fuzzy nudged Cinnabun and indicated the door, which was slowly closing. "Let's go!" The two of them blasted out from beneath the desk like their buns were on fire.

"There!" yelled Mossy Mustache. "Get 'em!"

He and Becca bent low, snatching at Fuzzy and Cinnabun. But when the two pets ran a crisscross pattern, the guards bumped heads and staggered apart.

Over the threshold and into the main hall ran Fuzzy and Cinnabun. The place was utter bedlam. Tour groups tangled, docents tried to keep order, and students scampered everywhere, squealing. In all the madness, nobody noticed two little rodents on a field trip.

The guards emerged and were immediately swamped by panicked people.

Cinnabun moved to hug the wall—the longer, safer route.

"Forget it!" Fuzzy shouted. "They wouldn't notice us if we were shooting off fireworks." He set a course directly for the open front doors, with the bunny right beside him.

Dodging and twisting to avoid clumsy human feet, the pets galloped for the exit, hoping against hope that

their ride was still there. When at last they burst outside, Fuzzy gave a great *wheek* of relief. A long yellow school bus waited at the curb.

But for how much longer?

He and Cinnabun jumped, scrambled, and tumbled down the stairs. As they drew closer, Fuzzy saw that most of the kids in the bus were on their feet, and that one of the teachers was leaning far out a window, snatching at something on the roof.

When they reached the bottom of the stairs, they found out what.

"Took you long enough!" squawked Sassafras from her perch atop the bus. She hopped just beyond the teacher's reach, and the kids hanging out the windows cheered. "Did you stop off for a nap and some cheese nibbles?"

"There were . . . complications," Fuzzy panted.

"Ain't that always the case," said the parakeet. "Luckily, I"—she bowed modestly—"am a master of distraction."

"That's an understatement," said Cinnabun.

She and Fuzzy hustled over to the open bus door. When he saw the height of the first step, Fuzzy blanched.

No way could he reach it. He was well and properly stuck.

"What's wrong, Brother Fuzzy?" asked the bunny.

"I, uh—you go ahead."

Cinnabun looked from the step to Fuzzy. Her dimples deepened. "Fiddlesticks," she said. "We go together, or not at all. May I give you a boost?"

Gratefully, he allowed her to help him up the steps. When they reached the top, he winced. "Sorry our field trip turned into such a disaster."

"Disaster?" The bunny surveyed the clamoring kids and the teacher finally carrying a grinning Sassafras into the bus. "Well, paint me green and call me a cucumber," she said. "What's an adventure without a little muss and fuss?"

CHAPTER 20

Grime and Punishment

Not until after the weekend could the pets meet up again. Miss Wills and the other fifth-grade teachers were convinced that someone had sneaked the animals onto her class's bus as a prank. The fact that they were never able to pin it on anyone didn't shake their belief. The pets said nothing, content to recover from their adventure.

On Monday of the following week, Fuzzy found himself slipping out of his cage and following his familiar route up the bookcase and into the dim crawl space. He couldn't help feeling a few butterflies in his stomach. Yes, he had led their first field trip and brought everyone home safely, but he wasn't sure how the other pets felt about the ruckus at the end.

Or about his mean trick on Cinnabun.

For all he knew, the rest of them could be planning to ban him from leading other field trips. And that would be a real shame. Because now that Fuzzy had tried the taste of freedom, he couldn't forget it. He loved his life in 5-B, sure. But he longed for new sights, new adventures.

As he approached their clubhouse, golden light shone upward where the ceiling tile lay askew. The babble of voices arose from below. The other pets had already arrived.

Fuzzy paused at the edge of the plank. He dusted off his fur and stood up straight. No matter what awaited him, he would make a dignified entrance. That at least he could control.

Climbing onto the board, he decided to steal a page from Cinnabun's book. He would glide down, just like the rabbit had. Fuzzy planted his feet, struck a pose, and let gravity do the rest.

Things went pretty well until he was a third of the way down, in full view of the group. Then, everything started speeding up. He slid faster and faster still, windmilling his arms to keep his balance.

"Whooooah!"

Finally, Fuzzy lost the battle with gravity. Down he toppled, rolling head over heels, off the plank and into a dirty pillow.

Poomph!

Dust billowed around him and he coughed.

Igor clapped sarcastically. "Well, he didn't stick the landing. But I'd still give him an eight-point-two for entertainment value."

Fuzzy felt his ears prickle with embarrassment. He raised his face from the pillow. "What?"

Marta helped him to his feet. "Igor waxed the plank. Everybody took a tumble but Cinnabun."

Of course, thought Fuzzy, brushing himself off.

"And me," said Sassafras, preening her wing feathers. "Because I'm naturally graceful."

"And you flew," said Luther.

"That too," the parakeet agreed, grinning.

Pounding her gavel on the presidential podium, President Cinnabun called the meeting to order. "Let's begin, y'all. Shall we?"

The pets settled into a rough semicircle around the Shakespeare book, and the bunny peered down at them.

"First, I'd like to address old business," said Cinnabun. "Do any of y'all have any comments on last week's field trip?"

Fuzzy gulped and looked around the circle.

"It felt a little risky," said Marta. "If I never have another close call like I did in Fuzzy's classroom, I'll be a happy tortoise."

He winced. She had a good point. "Sorry."

"I've never been so scared in all my life," said Mistletoe.

Fuzzy grimaced. "Sorry again."

"And the food," said Igor, "was definitely second-rate. Not a green bean or snap pea to be found."

"Okay, I get it!" Fuzzy burst out. "It was a terrible field trip, and you all had an awful time. Wiggling whiskers!"

Mistletoe frowned. "I didn't have an awful time."

"Me neither," said Marta. "In fact, I've never had such an exciting adventure."

"You what?" said Fuzzy.

The mouse thumped her chest proudly. "And I never knew I could cause such a big distraction. I'm resourceful, I am."

"I learned things about myself I never knew before," said Cinnabun. "And what's more, it was an amazing experience—obstacles and all."

Fuzzy's throat felt tighter than a teacher's budget. He glanced over at Igor.

"Ah, it wasn't half-bad," the iguana said. "But I really do want some better snacks."

The other pets chuckled. "And who would like to go on another field trip sometime?" asked Cinnabun. "Not tomorrow, you understand, but sometime?"

Fuzzy looked around. One by one, every pet's paw, wing, or tail raised into the air. His eyes felt misty.

"Of course," said the bunny, "Brother Fuzzy did play rather a mean trick on me."

His gut clenched. Fuzzy studied the floor, wishing he could disappear into it. "I'm so, so sorry."

"Bless your heart," said Cinnabun. "But I reckon there's only one way to make up for it."

He nodded. "I know. I should leave the club and never come back."

"What?!" Mistletoe and the other pets protested.

"Not quite what I had in mind," said the bunny, reaching behind the podium for the oversized pink ribbon. "As his punishment, Brother Fuzzy must wear this ribbon and sing three verses of 'Boom-Chicka-Smooch'!"

The club dissolved in laughter as Fuzzy donned the dreaded ribbon and sang the obnoxious song, ears burning. "Louder!" squawked Sassafras. "We can't hear you!"

At last, he finished. The chuckles died away and Fuzzy ditched the ribbon.

"If there's no more old business?" Cinnabun asked. The pets shook their heads. "Then I have some new business for the club."

"Let 'er rip, Missy Miss," said Luther.

The bunny allowed herself a small smile. "I would like to nominate Brother Fuzzy as the Class Pets Club's new director of adventure."

"I second that," said Marta.

"All in favor?" asked Cinnabun.

"Aye!" everyone roared. Fuzzy's heart swelled, and his smile threatened to wrap around his head.

Cinnabun nodded. "Then the motion is carried." She banged the gavel. "Now I have just one question for our new director of adventure."

"Yes?" asked Fuzzy.

"Where," said the bunny, dimples sprouting anew, "will he take us next?"

Read on for a sneak peek at

CLASS PETS

#2: Fuzzy Takes Charge

The substitute's knuckles tightened around the ruler. He glowered at Jake for a moment, then turned and stalked up to Fuzzy's cage. Wielding the straightedge like a sword, Mr. Brittle growled, "You had better mind your manners, mister. I hear that in Peru, they *eat* guinea pigs."

Suffering mange mites! Shocked to the core, Fuzzy shrank behind his igloo. He heard students gasp.

Mr. Brittle wheeled on the class. "Enough time-wasting. We will begin our lessons, and I warn you"—again, he brandished the ruler—"you had better not try any tricks with me, you little snots. Because I. Hate. Tricks." On each of his last three words, the sub smacked the straightedge on Fuzzy's table. *Whack-whack-whack!*

Nerves frazzled, Fuzzy huddled behind one of his blocks and watched the substitute sneer and bully his way through the morning. One whole week of this? Fuzzy didn't think he could stand it. More important, he didn't think his students could stand it.

Somebody had to do something. The kids were powerless, so that meant *he* had to do something.

But what?

Fuzzy didn't know. Still, as he brooded, gnawing on the corner of his block, one thing became crystal clear.

Whatever the method, whatever it took, this sub must go.